"Had Joel already told you about me?"

"Of course not," Lindsay replied.

"You see, I know all about you," Marilyn said with obvious satisfaction. "I was relieved when you resigned, rather than my having to ask Joel to get rid of you."

Lindsay stiffened. "You seem very confident."

Much as she hated to admit it, Lindsay was afraid Marilyn had more influence with Joel than she'd ever had. He seemed to see the other woman every day, and although it didn't seem to be making him happy, he kept going back for more.

"I don't think you quite understand, Lindsay. I still use my professional name of Mills when I'm modeling, but my name actually became Sutherland seven years ago."

Lindsay was dumbstruck. Although it did seem to make Joel's aversion to marriage more understandable, she [...] Joel capable of such [...]

Books by Carole Mortimer

HARLEQUIN PRESENTS

These books may be available at your local bookseller.

Don't miss any of our special offers. Write to us at the following address for information on our newest releases.

Harlequin Reader Service
P.O. Box 52040, Phoenix, AZ   85072-2040
Canadian address: P.O. Box 2800, Postal Station A,
5170 Yonge St., Willowdale, Ont.   M2N 6J3

CAROLE MORTIMER

tempestuous affair

Harlequin Books

TORONTO • NEW YORK • LONDON
AMSTERDAM • PARIS • SYDNEY • HAMBURG
STOCKHOLM • ATHENS • TOKYO • MILAN

For
John and Matthew

Harlequin Presents first edition June 1985
ISBN 0-373-10797-8

Original hardcover edition published in 1984
by Mills & Boon Limited

CHAPTER ONE

'LINDSAY? Lindsay, open this door, damn you!'

She wasn't distressed or shocked by the cold anger in Joel's voice as he shouted through the thickness of her closed flat door; she had been expecting him, and this reaction. She hadn't known at what time, or even precisely what day, but she had known he would come here as soon as he returned from his business trip. Maybury would have told him, of course. And he was far from pleased—as she had known he would be.

'Lindsay,' his voice had lowered now, becoming cajoling. 'Let me in and we can talk.'

Talk. It had never got them anywhere in the past, and she doubted very much that it would get them anywhere now.

'Lindsay, please!'

His pleading was her undoing. Joel Sutherland never pleaded for anything, least of all for a woman to talk to him; there were so many others who were only too willing to do a lot more than that! The fact that he was pleading with her now only enhanced how desperate he was that they should at least talk.

She moved forward with naturally graceful movements, the golden hair level with her jaw framing the beauty of her face, a face that until minutes ago had been ravaged with indecision. But none of that showed now, in her green almond-shaped eyes surrounded by light brown lashes, her nose small and pert, her perfectly formed bow of a mouth made to look even more provocative by the deep rose-coloured lipgloss she wore. She had the face and body of a model, but more intelligence than to involve herself in such a precarious and shortlived profession. The laughter lines beside her eyes seemed to indicate that she enjoyed what she did with her life, and that life liked her too.

But she wasn't enjoying her life right now, as she opened the door apprehensively to Joel, knowing from experience that the next half an hour or so wasn't going to be pleasant. She hadn't been his secretary for the past year without realising that, and she knew that when things were going well for him no one could be more charming, but when things were going badly . . .! Objects had been known to fly across the room at such times. And she had a feeling this was going to be one of those times!

Joel didn't wait for her to do more than unlock the door, pushing it open forcefully as he strode angrily into the room, looking about him with narrowed eyes, as if he hadn't expected her to be alone. He turned back to look at her as she slowly closed the door. 'Where is he?' he bit out.

Her frown of puzzlement was completely genuine; she had no idea what he was talking about. 'Who?'

'Roger Hillier,' he dismissed with impatient anger. 'Or am I too early?' He glanced at the gold watch on his wrist. 'Yes, I suppose I am, he doesn't usually crawl out of bed until dusk,' he derided with contempt.

Lindsay took a few minutes to drink in her fill of the man who held her heart in the palm of his hand. He still affected her as deeply as he had the first moment she had seen him, still made her heart flutter in her chest, her palms suddenly feel damp. At thirty-four, twelve years her senior, his dark hair showed not even a sprinkling of grey, growing thick and black in unruly disarray, in a habitual state of having those lean sensitive hands run through it. His eyes were his most dominant feature, golden when he was elated or pleased, tawny when he was angry. There was no doubt about what colour they were now! A long thin nose jutted out above the full sensuality of his mouth, his jaw was square and firm. It wasn't a handsome face by any stretch of the imagination; what it was was strong, telling of the power he wielded day after day with the expertise of his camera. Unlike many of his contemporaries he chose to shun the use of casual denims and shirts for the main part, claiming that his clients could have more confidence in a man who didn't look like a reject from the sixties! The success of his photographic agency seemed to indicate he was right. The fact that he looked his best in the three-piece suits he favoured, the jackets fitting over the broadness of his shoulders, the waistcoat buttoned tautly over his flat stomach, the trousers fitting snugly to his narrow hips and long muscular legs, helped, of course.

He was wearing one of those suits now, a brown one with contrasting cream shirt, his hair slightly longer than he usually wore it after a month away from his regular hairdresser. Joel looked everything that he was, powerful, successful, dynamic—and even after six months of living with him Lindsay was no nearer to knowing his complexities, let alone understanding them!

'So when is Hillier due to arrive?' His mouth was twisted derisively now.

'Why?'

'So I can have the pleasure of breaking his neck when he does, of course!' he rasped, his eyes glittering.

Lindsay sat down with a calmness she had learnt was essential when dealing with a man like Joel. Ranting and raving back at him was exactly what he wanted, especially when he was spoiling for a fight, like now.

The pale green silk dress she wore fell silkily about her long legs as she sat, its shirtwaister style flattering to her slender figure, a bow-neck taking away any plainness in the style of the dress. Joel always liked her to dress in clothes that weren't too fussy or frilly, and over the past months she had bought her wardrobe with him in mind.

'Why should you imagine Roger is coming here at all?' she asked coolly, her gaze steady.

'Because he's been after you for months to go and work for him,' Joel scowled, pacing the room.

'Is that why you persuaded me to live with you?' she asked with bitterness.

'I'm not that desperate to keep a secretary!' he snapped.

'And I'm not that desperate to find myself another job!' Her eyes flashed warningly, deeply green.

Joel stopped his pacing long enough to look down at her, frowning darkly, the tawny eyes showing his confusion. 'Does that mean you haven't left me?'

'It means I'm still your secretary,' she told him pointedly. 'For as long as you want me to be.'

'And moving back to this apartment? God, I didn't even know you had kept up the lease,' he bit out.

Lindsay shrugged with a casualness she was far from feeling. 'You never asked.'

'I assumed—But it never pays to assume with you, does it!' he accused angrily. 'I *assumed* you would be at my apartment waiting for me when I got back today, and look how wrong I was about that!' He glared at her fiercely.

'It may have escaped your notice,' she was still outwardly calm, although she knew from experience how quickly that could change, Joel being able to fire her temper as no one else had ever done, 'but the six months ended while you were away.'

'It didn't "escape my notice" at all,' he said furiously. 'It just never occurred to me that you would leave.'

'That was the agreement when I first moved in with you,' she reminded him.

His eyes gleamed with as yet suppressed fury. 'The agreement was that we would reassess the situation at the end of six months.' His voice was controlled, too controlled not to be dangerous.

'As you weren't here I did that on my own.'

'And moved out!'

'Yes.'

'*Why?*' he demanded to know. 'That's what I can't understand.' Lindsay shrugged. 'It was for the best.'

'*Whose* best?'

'Mine,' she told him with simplicity.

He seemed to pale, as if she had inflicted a deep hurt on him. But she knew that wouldn't be true. Joel would be the first to admit he didn't have a heart to inflict pain to!

'And what about me?' he asked quietly. 'I certainly didn't want you to leave.'

'I know that,' she nodded.

'Then *why did you?*' His hands clenched into fists at his sides. 'The last six months with you have been the best time of my life. I thought you felt the same way, in fact I would swear that you did,' he added challengingly.

She moistened her lips with the pink tip of her tongue. The trouble with that last accusation was that she did. Living with Joel, being with him day and night for the last six months, had been the most wonderful six months she had ever known—and they had also been the most heartbreaking! She loved a man who refused to believe there was such an emotion, who scorned at those who did, so how could she ever know true happiness with him?

Oh, she had known all this about him six months ago, had been sure she could convince him otherwise when so many others had failed to do so, had moved in with him because she believed that. On the surface they were happy together, Joel being content to have her in his office with him every day, and in his bed every night, never letting her fall asleep without showing her very convincingly how much he desired and wanted her. And she had been content with those things too for a while, until it became obvious that it would never change, that Joel would only ever want her as a live-in lover and nothing more.

The only thing he had ever shared with her had been his work; his family and his life before he met her a closed book. The latter it had been easy to find out about; he was a world-renowned photographer and the press had reported his much-varied love-life the last five or six years. About his family she only knew that his parents lived in the south of England, and that he hadn't visited them once while they lived together. It wasn't much information to have accumulated about the man she lived with so intimately, and even that hadn't been told to her by Joel himself. He was a very private man, so private he didn't allow even those who cared about him close to him.

She still loved him, that would never change, but

she wanted more from him, *needed* more. And he just didn't have it to give. She didn't like admitting she had failed, although she knew her mother would be relieved, never having approved of the relationship from the first. Her older sister had been the only one who understood and encouraged what she was trying to do; Judi was always there to listen when Lindsay needed someone to talk to. And that had been often since she had known Joel, the first rosy glow of being with him quickly deteriorating to uncertainty, and finally fear, a fear that had been proven when it became obvious he couldn't love her.

'I did,' she began. 'I——'

'Did?' he repeated harshly. 'What's that supposed to mean? Either you've liked living with me or you haven't!'

'I have. But——'

'And you can't deny that physically we're perfect together,' he added determinedly.

Lindsay blushed under his narrow-eyed stare. There was no denying what had been obvious from their first night together, when as a complete novice when it came to making love she had been initiated into a world of sensuality with a tenderness and an expertise that had meant she knew none of the pain she had associated with that dreaded 'first time'. Joel had been elated at the idea of being her first lover, and had gone on to teach her every physical intimacy there was between a man and a woman. That part of their relationship had only got better as time went on, even Lindsay's uncertainties about their future together not affecting that.

'You know we are,' she mumbled. 'But——'

'Then what are you doing here?' he demanded to know forcefully. 'And why did you never mention it to me when I telephoned you at the office? Maybury said you moved out a couple of days after I went to America.'

'That's right, I did. And if you'd ever called me at the apartment in the evenings Maybury would have told you I'd gone.' Joel's manservant had had instructions to do just that. Only Joel never telephoned her in the evenings; he had been so sure that she would be waiting for him that he hadn't found out until his return that she had flown their love-nest.

Love-nest! That was a lie in itself. She loved, Joel just wanted, only she had been too much in love to see that was all it was. Joel had her to run his office efficiently, Maybury to see that his apartment was kept clean and comfortable, and that his meals were served when and if he wanted them. The only thing left for the woman in his life to do was share his bed, and after a while that could become a little degrading. They didn't share their thoughts, and they didn't share their dreams, even Lindsay's usually open manner learning caution after Joel's first half a dozen lukewarm responses to her mentions of her family and friends. He didn't want to meet either, feeling it would be highly hypocritical when most of them disapproved of their relationship. And maybe it would have been, but it would also have made Lindsay extremely happy!

Most of her family and friends would tell her she was a fool, that everything she now knew about Joel, his independence from all emotional relationships, his arrogance when he felt he had been slighted, his cold-blooded disregard for anyone's feelings but his own, had all been there for her to see before she took the irrevocable step of moving in with him. And she did know it now, to her cost.

Joel looked even more angry than ever. 'You aren't telling me you left me simply because I didn't have the time to call you in the evenings?' He sounded disgusted.

Her eyes flashed. 'I hope you know me better than that,' she said stiffly.

'I'm beginning to think I don't know you at all,' he ground out.

'I left you because it was time to leave.' She refused to be antagonised into losing her temper. 'We want different things from life,' she told him wearily.

'I want *you*!'

'But you don't love me.'

His eyes narrowed to wary amber slits. 'You knew that from the beginning, I told you then how it would be.'

She deserved this, although she hadn't expected Joel to be the first to tell her, 'I told you so'. 'Yes,' she sighed acknowledgement of his honesty about his feeling from the first.

'But you expected more.' His mouth twisted contemptuously.

She flinched at the derision in his voice. She hadn't been expecting a belated declaration of love from him, not even for him to ask her to go back to him, but neither had she wanted him to scorn her desire, her need, for affection. He had never scorned her before, and it hurt.

'I didn't expect it,' she replied quietly. 'Although I wouldn't have repulsed it either,' she added huskily.

'Lindsay?'

She stood up impatiently, her hands tightly clasped together. 'We agreed to try living together, to see how it worked out. As far as I'm concerned it didn't. So let it be the end of it.'

Joel swung her round, his hands rough on her arms. 'Do you love me, Lindsay?'

Tears swam in her eyes as she looked up at him, so much taller than her despite her own considerable height. 'And if I do?' she asked softly.

His face became a shuttered mask, his eyes bleak, his hands falling away from her as he stepped away. 'Love was never part of our agreement.'

'Then it's as well I *don't* love you, isn't it?' She looked at him with challenge in her eyes, knowing by the narrowed suspicion of his that he wasn't sure whether to believe her or not. Pride came to her rescue as she sensed his indecision. 'I only made a supposition, Joel,' she dismissed lightly. 'I don't love you or any other man. But I do want more from a relationship than you can give me.'

His mouth was a thin angry line. 'Such as?' he rasped.

She shrugged, putting her hands in the hip pockets of her dress so that he shouldn't see them shaking. 'Like sharing, giving, maybe even a little fun.' She met his gaze steadily. 'You're so intent on keeping your emotions in check that you've forgotten even how to have that! Do you realise that the only times we've been out you've taken me to respectable restaurants or equally respectable clubs?'

'Would you rather I'd taken you to *un*respectable ones?' he demanded exasperatedly.

'You're missing my point, Joel,' she sighed.

'I'm not sure *you* even know what that is!'

She blushed at his scorn, knowing he would never understand what she was trying to tell him, his emotions so firmly controlled that he couldn't understand her need to share laughter and tears with him. 'Okay, so maybe those two examples weren't very good ones,' she admitted. 'All I'm trying to explain is that you never *shared* things with me. You shut me out of everything but your bed. And although that may be enough for some women it isn't for me!'

'Isn't it?'

Lindsay swallowed hard at the dangerous softness of his voice, her senses instantly alerted. And she was right to feel nervous as she was pulled back against him, his arms about her waist as his lips nuzzled against her throat.

She groaned as the usual lethargy possessed her when he took her in his arms, trembling as his hands moved up to cup her breasts over the green silky dress, her nipples flowering to his touch after the weeks without him. He knew her so well, knew that her breasts were the most sensitive part of her body, gently squeezing her nipples between thumbs and fingers with just enough pressure to cause the pleasure-pain that made her weak at the knees.

She turned eagerly into his arms, needing to feel his lips on hers, wanting so much more than he was giving.

'You see, Lindsay?' He looked down at her triumphantly. 'This is all that really counts.'

She was too aroused to be alarmed by his obvious satisfaction in her instantaneous response, already able to see them together in her imagination, their legs entwined, their naked bodies pressed together as they gave each other fulfilment that went beyond even the imagination.

All her plans to remain immune to him were forgotten as he plundered her mouth with ruthless intent, his fingers nimbly releasing the buttons down the front of her dress, smoothing the material down her arms to fall unheeded about her narrow waist. He cupped her bared breasts in his hands, his thumbtips moving across the already hardened tips to cause spasms of delight to course through her body, his tongue now penetrating the warm cavern of her mouth with rhythmic eroticism.

As he bent his head to claim first one nipple into his mouth with a sucking motion, and then the other, Lindsay's fingers became entangled in the dark unruliness of his hair, pressing him against her as his tongue flicked erotically over the hardened nipple, barely aware of him unbuttoning his own clothing until his mouth moved back to hers, the heated dampness of his chest crushed abrasively against her extremely sensitive breasts.

'Touch me, Lindsay,' he encouraged with a groan. 'Touch me the way I've dreamt of you touching me the last four weeks I've been away from you!'

His eyes were golden, evidence of how deeply aroused he was, and as her hand moved down to his thigh between them she could feel the physical evidence of his desire leaping against her. It had been a long time for both of them, and she could tell Joel was fast approaching the point of no return.

A sudden fear entered her at how close they were to making love, knowing that if they did that Joel would be able to persuade her to move back in with him, once again under his terms and conditions. No matter how much pain it cost her to do so, she knew she had to stop him now, before it was too late.

Her hands came up to push at his shoulders, as ineffectual as she had known they would be against his superior strength, although his eyes glittered dangerously as he sensed her withdrawal, his mouth claiming hers in a kiss of sensual demand, willing her not to turn away from him, his mouth becoming savage on hers as he sensed he was failing to convince her.

His head was raised sharply as he tasted the salt of her tears on their lips, his expression harsh as he looked down at her grief-stricken face. 'Why are you crying?' he rasped. 'You've never cried before!'

She could see he despised the weakness, that he preferred his life to be uncomplicated by such emotions, and she pulled her dress back up her arms over her nakedness, very much aware of the nipples still pressed against the material in obvious arousal as he rebuttoned it for her.

'Lindsay, tell me why you were crying?' he demanded at her continued silence.

She looked at him with tear-wet eyes. 'It's over between us, can't you see that?' she choked.

His mouth twisted with derision. 'You responded to me just now, you know you did.'

'I told you, *it isn't enough!*'

Something flickered deep in his eyes, a mixture of contempt and pity. 'Why is it women always demand more?' he derided bitingly. 'I've given you all my time and loyalty. There's been no one else for me since you moved in with me six months ago, and God knows I've had the opportunity!'

She knew that. A man as attractive as Joel, surrounded as he was every day by beautiful and desirable women, was sure to receive plenty of invitations. 'It's never been a question of that and you know it.' She had never had reason to question his fidelity to her, knew that if he had wanted to be unfaithful to the tenuous relationship they had then he would simply tell her so; the one thing she knew she could always expect and get from him was honesty. No, she knew there had been no one else, and perhaps that in itself was a commitment from a man who had previously lived with no woman but made love to many. Only it still wasn't enough for her.

'I'm sorry,' she told him flatly.

'Sorry!' he scorned. 'For what? For leaving me? Or for leaving at a time when you knew I couldn't stop you? Because you know damn well I would have done, don't you?' he accused fiercely.

She had known, and he was right, she had only found the strength to leave because he was away and unable to stop her. She would never have found the courage to come right out against him. 'All that's irrelevant now, Joel,' she dismissed, running her fingertips through the silky tangle of her hair, feeling it fall back into style against her cheek. 'I have left, and I have no intention of ever coming back.'

His eyes had narrowed to tawny slits. 'So where does that leave us now?'

She swallowed hard. 'I think that's entirely up to you, don't you?' she said quietly.

He thrust his hands into his trousers pockets, his shirt and waistcoat still unbuttoned, falling open to his waist. 'You aren't involved with Hillier?' he demanded harshly.

Lindsay frowned at his persistence in believing she was. 'I've only ever seen him on the few occasions he's been to the studio.'

'When he made it perfectly obvious how attracted he is to you,' Joel scowled his displeasure.

With any other man she would have put his behaviour down to jealousy, but with Joel she knew that wasn't so; he was never jealous or possessive, believing in total personal freedom for everyone. No, he was just annoyed at the thought of possibly losing his secretary. 'Roger is like that with all women.' She dismissed, with a smile, the young photographer who had helped Joel in the past, flirtatious with every woman he came into contact with, regardless of age or beauty, and it didn't mean a thing.

'Since he set up on his own he's been looking for a secretary/receptionist.' Joel still didn't look convinced.

'Well, he's never mentioned that to me,' she shook her head.

'He's mentioned it to me!' he rasped. 'And I warned him off you. It took me long enough to find you!'

Lindsay stiffened as he confirmed what she had always thought to be true, that she was more important to him as a secretary than as the woman he lived with! 'I've told you,' she said coldly, 'I'm still your secretary.'

'For as long as I want you to be,' he scorned.

'Yes,' she nodded.

'I want you back where you belong!' he grated, glaring at her. 'At the apartment.'

'I belong here, this is my home.'

'Your home is with me!'

She moistened suddenly dry lips. 'Joel, I——'

'I'm not going to beg,' he cut in angrily. 'If I leave without you now I'll never ask you again.'

She knew he meant it, knew he possessed a stubbornness that was equal to none, that pride often held him back from asking anything of anyone. 'I'll see you at nine o'clock on Monday morning,' she told him softly, seeing the anger flare up anew in his eyes, knowing at that moment that he really hadn't believed when he came here tonight that he would have to leave without her.

'Damn you, then, Lindsay Pope!' he bit out furiously, striding towards the door. 'I never ask a woman for a second time!' he warned her raggedly.

She looked at him with unflinching green eyes. 'I'm counting on it.'

The apartment reverberated from the slam he gave the door as he left, and Lindsay winced from the aftershock, sitting down weakly in one of the armchairs. Whatever Joel had made of her last comment she knew that if he persisted in chasing after her she would eventually have given in. And that would just take her back to the same situation she had needed so desperately to escape from.

But it hadn't been easy to say no to him, and she shook from the need to run after him and tell him it had all been a mistake. But common sense held her back—that, and the knowledge that she couldn't suffer through another six months of knowing she meant nothing to him only to have *him* then turn around and ask her to leave because he was bored with her.

But it was going to be far from easy working, and seeing him every day, in future!

'All right, Lindsay,' her sister Judi, the older by two years, encouraged. 'You can tell me what's troubling you now that Mike's gone out.'

Lindsay had driven down to spend the day with her family at the house in Cambridgeshire, only to find her mother out for the morning at church, and her tormenting younger brother Mike refusing to leave the house in case he missed any of their gossip, finally being persuaded to do so by a couple of his friends who called round.

She sighed at her sister's perception. 'You have to know some time, Judi. I've left Joel.'

Her sister frowned. She was as blonde and pretty as Lindsay, with an underlying sadness always present in her hazel eyes. 'I thought you were happy together,' she prompted gently.

'*Joel* was,' Lindsay corrected pointedly. 'As long as I didn't make any emotional demands on him.'

Judi's expression was full of compassion. 'And you made some, hmm?'

'I had more sense than to try!' she sighed. 'It just didn't work out, Judi,' she explained in a stronger voice. 'I thought I could be the one to change his mind about love and marriage. It must be the biggest deception a woman can give herself,' she added self-derisively.

'It was worth a try when you love him so much,' her sister comforted.

Lindsay's mouth twisted wryly. 'I'm sure Mother doesn't think so!'

'You mustn't mind her,' Judi said gently. 'She doesn't understand anything except marriage, it's just the way she expects things should be.'

Their mother had been left a widow five years ago, had enjoyed a happy married life with their father for over twenty years, and she just couldn't understand— or forgive—Lindsay for simply moving in with Joel the way that she had. Nothing much had been said, the disapproval being mainly silent, but Lindsay had been as aware of it as if her mother had shouted it from the rooftops.

She had tried to persuade Joel to visit her mother, sure that once the two of them met they would get on together. Joel had refused, and her mother had been unenthusiastic about the idea too, always complaining about their living arrangements when Lindsay visited home alone. To make matters worse Mike considered her living with Joel was really great, further encouraging her mother's disapproval. If she needed any encouraging!

'Do *you* think I was wrong, Judi?' she voiced her uncertainty to her sister.

'Not when you loved him so much,' Judi shook her head.

'But you and Jonathan never—I mean——'

'No, we didn't,' Judi confirmed hollowly. 'But I'll always wish that we had.'

Lindsay's eyes widened. 'You will?'

Judi nodded. 'But he refused to once he knew how ill he was, said he didn't want us to have any accidents that would maybe prevent my marrying after—after he was gone. As if I'll ever want to marry anyone else now that he's dead!'

Judi's fiancé Jonathan had died two years ago of leukaemia, leaving everyone who knew and loved him devastated by his loss. Judi had never recovered from losing her childhood sweetheart so tragically, the two of them having dated since they were at school together, and Lindsay now felt guilty about introducing a subject that could still upset her sister so much.

'I'm sorry, love,' one of her hands covered Judi's. 'I shouldn't have probed.'

The hazel eyes were shadowed with memories. 'It's a relief to be able to talk about him, actually. Mother avoids the subject as if he never existed. And she keeps bringing up the fact that she doesn't have any grandchildren yet.'

Lindsay's mouth twisted wryly. 'Then I must be a double disappointment to her.'

Judi smiled comfortingly. 'I think we're all a disappointment to her—even poor Mike gets nagged about how irresponsible he is, and he's only eighteen!'

Lindsay shook her head. 'I can't understand why you continue to stay here. Mother certainly doesn't appreciate you.' Lindsay had taken the first opportunity she could to escape her mother's oppressive attitude after their father died, having moved to London as soon as she had the job to do so.

'I don't mind,' Judi smiled again. 'My job is here, and most of my friends are too. And when it gets too much for me at home I can always go up to London for a few days to visit my notorious sister!' she added mischievously.

Lindsay grimaced. 'I dread to think what Mother's going to say when I tell her I've left Joel.'

'Do you have to?' her sister sympathised.

'I suppose I should,' she pulled a face at the thought.

As it turned out her mother was the one to introduce the subject. 'I telephoned you several times last week.' She looked at Lindsay accusingly, a small plump woman with prematurely grey hair who didn't look as if she could possibly be the mother of such a tall family. 'That man Maybury kept telling me you weren't at home. I would have thought, with—with Mr Sutherland away,' she even had difficulty mentioning his name, 'that you would have stayed in during the evenings. I know the two of you have an—unorthodox arrangement,' she added haughtily, 'but I'm sure he wouldn't like the idea of you going out without him like that.'

Lindsay shot Judi a resigned look. 'I wasn't at the apartment, Mother, because I've moved out,' she told her bluntly, knowing there was no other way.

Pale green eyes sharpened suspiciously. 'Moved out? What do you mean?'

She sighed, aware that her young brother was all ears as they sat around the luncheon table. 'I've moved back to my own apartment,' she explained.

'Why?'

Her brows rose at her mother's vehemence. 'I thought you'd be pleased by the news.'

'Pleased!' her mother echoed shrilly. 'You disgrace the whole family by moving in with that—that *man*,' she amended at Lindsay's frowning look, 'and now you expect me to be thrilled that you've moved out again!'

'Yes.'

'Well, I'm not.' She stood up noisily, leaving her meal only half eaten. 'You'll be ruined by this, Lindsay,' she warned agitatedly. 'The whole family has been ruined by your selfishness!' and she stormed from the room.

Lindsay was trembling in reaction to the explosion, giving a shaky laugh to break the tense silence. 'So much for motherly love,' she derided.

Judi gave a regretful sigh. 'She's just surprised, she expected you to marry Joel.'

'She wasn't the only one,' Lindsay choked.

'Does this mean you won't let me look around Joel's photographic studio?' Mike put in disappointedly.

'Mike!' Judi reproved him frowningly. 'Can't you see Lindsay is upset?' she glared at him.

'But she was the one who left him——'

'Oh, be quiet, Mike!' Judi snapped with uncharacteristic sharpness. 'Maybe when you're a bit more mature you'll understand.'

He stood up. 'I wish you'd all realise that I *am* mature!' He slammed out of the room disgustedly.

Lindsay pulled a rueful face. 'I think his pride is injured.'

'Then he should think a bit more before he speaks. Don't worry,' Judi assured her as she still looked concerned, 'I'll talk to him later.'

'And Mother?'

Her sister shrugged. 'She may take a little longer coming round, but she will eventually.'

'I needed her understanding now, not eventually!' Lindsay said with bitterness.

Judi sighed. 'I'm sorry, love.'

So was she, sorry she had ever told her mother about Joel. And she needn't have done; she could have lied to the whole family, could have simply told them she was changing apartments, and they would have been none the wiser. But she hadn't; she had been honest about her actions, had borne her mother's disapproval without demur. It would have been better for everyone, including herself, if she had never heard of Joel Sutherland.

And yet as she lay alone in her bed that night she couldn't help thinking about him, wondering if he too were lying alone in the huge double bed they had shared for so long. Somehow she doubted it; he had never wasted time in replacing his women in the past.

God, how she ached to be with him now, wished she could go back six months to when she had first moved in with him, could live that time all over again.

Joel had been escorting one of his models for several weeks when she first went to work for him, a beautiful redhead who had lasted only two more weeks before she was replaced by an even more beautiful brunette.

After that Lindsay had watched a stream of lovely women enter and leave his life, none of them touching him emotionally, although several of them claimed to have fallen in love with him, a couple of them crying on Lindsay's shoulder when she told them she had strict instructions from Joel not to let them into his studio or put their calls through. Their replacement would usually shortly be replaced herself, with the same emotional result.

At first Lindsay had watched this succession of beautiful women with amusement, and then with dismay as she realised she had joined their ranks and fallen in love with Joel herself. She had panicked then, handing in her notice, sure she would get over him if she didn't have to see him every day, knowing that she would mean no more to him than just being his secretary. But Joel had other ideas; he invited her out to dinner with the supposed intention of talking her into changing her mind about leaving. Dinner had progressed to a quiet club Joel knew, the two of them talking as they had never talked before, Joel kissing her goodnight after taking her home, a light promising kiss that made her ache for more. When he had invited her out the next evening neither of them had mentioned the fact that she had intended leaving his employment. Joel's goodnight kiss was more demanding this time; the two of them being completely alone in her apartment, although he took it no further than a kiss.

Over the next week their relationship developed rapidly from that of employer and employee, although once he realised she was still a virgin Joel refrained from forcing a conclusion to the rapidly spiralling sexual tension that now existed between them. Lindsay kept waiting for the axe to fall on their relationship, knowing that Joel had never settled for less than a full physical commitment before. But he had brought to an end the tense frustration in a way she had never expected, by asking her to move into his apartment with him on a trial basis.

She knew he had never done anything like that before, preferring to remain at his apartment while his women stayed in theirs. A living together arrangement was far from what she wanted, but the mere fact that Joel had never lived with anyone before gave her hope that they would eventually have a permanent future together.

She should have known better! Joel always treated her well, never demanded anything of her, respected her independence from him at all times. And of course that was part of the trouble. A man in love would have wanted her to be a little more dependent on him than she had been.

Maybe she *was* back to where she had been six months ago, after all. Despite what she had told Joel she couldn't continue to work for him. She only wished now that she hadn't let herself be persuaded out of that decision last time!

CHAPTER TWO

'Great,' snapped Joel with sarcasm, waving Lindsay's letter of resignation about in his hand. 'Just great! Your loyalty when I'm tied up in this contract for Reader is incredible!' He glared down at her.

Joel had been in his studio when she arrived at work half an hour ago, and the first thing she had done after checking the post had been to type out her letter of resignation, putting it in with the letters she had taken in to him a short time ago. His reaction was to be expected.

'I thought you went to America to complete that contract,' she frowned.

'I did,' he scowled, looking as if last night hadn't agreed with him either, whether he had slept alone or not. 'He liked the photographs so much he wants me to do the promotional shots on the new cosmetic range they have coming out,' he told her grudgingly. 'I've spent most of the last month trying to find the right model.'

Lindsay felt a flash of jealousy for all the beautiful women he would have seen the last month.

'None of them were right for the cosmetics,' he added mockingly as he saw her pensive expression.

'Did you test them all personally?' she heard herself ask waspishly.

'Photographically?' he drawled tauntingly, his eyebrows raised mockingly. 'Yes.'

She mentally berated herself for showing her

jealousy so plainly, knowing Joel was aware of exactly how she felt, that he was elated by it. Damn!

'Regretting your decision, Lindsay?' He sat on the edge of her desk, dangerously close, his tangy aftershave discernible to her. 'It isn't too late to change your mind, you know,' he encouraged throatily.

'My notice stands, thank you.' She was deliberately obtuse, knowing that wasn't the decision he was talking about.

His eyes darkened to tawny slits, and he stood up, pushing her letter into the hip pocket of his trousers. 'Bring me in the file on all the models I've used the last five years,' he instructed her curtly.

Her brows rose. 'All of them?'

'That's what I said, didn't I?' he snapped.

'Yes . . .'

'Then do it,' he rasped rudely. 'And don't keep me waiting all day!' The door slammed after him as he went back into his studio.

'Was that the bastard I know and love?' drawled an amused voice from the doorway.

'Cally!' Lindsay cried excitedly, getting up to hug the newcomer enthusiastically. 'When did you get back to town?'

'Over the weekend,' the other woman smiled. 'I thought I'd look in on my tormentor of the last four years. How is he?' she asked lightly.

Lindsay gave a rueful grimace at the firmly closed studio door. 'As charming as usual!' she said dryly. 'But don't let's talk about Joel,' she dismissed abruptly. 'Tell me how you like married life.'

Cally Robin had been Joel's top model until two months ago when she had met, and as quickly married, an up-and-coming Member of Parliament, much to

the surprise of her friends, and much to the
annoyance of Joel when she informed him she was
giving up modelling to help her husband in his
career. Joel and Cally had had an affair once, years
ago, and Cally was one of the few women he now
called friend. Lindsay had been a little jealous of
their relationship to begin with, but as the warmth
and friendliness of Cally soon overflowed to her too
she had no reason to do so.

'I love it,' Cally answered, her blue eyes sparkling,
her red hair a glowing cloud about her shoulders.
'David has to be the most wonderful man in the
world,' she added dreamily.

'I thought he was rather handsome when I met him
at the wedding,' Lindsay smiled teasingly.

'Keep your hands off,' Cally warned jokingly. 'I
have enough trouble fighting off all his female
constituents, without having to worry about you too!
So what's wong with Joel?' she sobered. 'He sounded
as if he was being a bear.'

Lindsay shrugged. 'He's no worse than usual,' she
prevaricated, knowing that Joel hadn't been like this
with her since before she moved in with him.

'And heaven knows that's bad enough!' Cally
grimaced. 'What—or should I say who—has upset
him?'

Lindsay sighed. 'I have a feeling it was me.'

'Yes?' Blue eyes widened in surprise. 'Are you
telling me he still rants and raves at you?'

Lindsay stiffened, her expression uncertain. 'Still?'
she enquired softly.

Cally patted her hand understandingly. 'You
mustn't mind that I know the two of you are living
together—Joel just happened to let it slip one day,' she
explained gently.

'Oh,' said Lindsay dully. 'Then perhaps I should tell you that we aren't, not any longer.'

Cally frowned at this. 'Since when?'

'Since I moved out.'

'*You* did?' The other woman was obviously surprised that she had been the one to end the relationship. 'That must have been a surprise for poor Joel,' she added questioningly.

'You could say that,' Lindsay grimaced.

'Oh, I do,' Cally nodded, looking thoughtful. 'The way he was talking it was a permanent arrangement.'

'As permanent as anything can be with a man like Joel,' Lindsay derided.

'No, I mean it,' Cally said, perfectly seriously. 'I really thought this was "it" for him.'

'If you mean love, Cally, then you should know him better than that,' said Lindsay flatly.

'He still has that problem, hmm?' Cally nodded shrewdly.

Lindsay gave her a sharp, probing look. 'What problem?'

'He doesn't know how to accept or give love.'

Her expression was dejected. 'How can you accept or give something you don't know exists!'

'Oh, Lindsay,' Cally was all sympathy. 'Don't——'

'What the hell is delaying you, Lindsay?' Joel suddenly appeared in the studio doorway, his eyes narrowing as he saw Cally perched provocatively on the side of Lindsay's desk. 'I might have known you had something to do with it,' he snapped. 'What's wrong, has married life begun to pall already?' he taunted.

Cally stood up, smoothing down the skirt of her dress with deliberate slowness before walking over to kiss him lingeringly on the mouth, seeming immune to his glowing displeasure. 'Married life is wonderful,' she gave him a mocking sideways glance. 'I would highly recommend it.'

His mouth twisted. 'Then you must be one of the few people who do,' he derided. 'And after only two months I don't think you've had time to really speak with any authority.'

'Cynic!' she said goodnaturedly, used to his bad humour.

'Realist.' He shot Lindsay a telling glance. 'I simply don't have stars in my eyes about an institution that's been failing for years. I'd rather get myself certified!'

Lindsay blanched, knowing the last was being said for her benefit, that Joel was making it clear once again that he would never contemplate marriage, to anyone. And that wasn't fair, because she had never mentioned marriage to him.

'Keep on the way you are,' Cally drawled mockingly, 'and I might just do it for you.'

He looked down at her with narrowed tawny eyes. 'What do you mean?' he bit out.

'Lindsay tells me you're no longer living together,' she provoked. 'You have to be insane to have let her escape.'

'Cally——'

'It was Lindsay's decision to leave,' Joel forcefully cut in on her dismayed response to Cally's taunting.

'Well, no one could think her insane for leaving you, darling,' Cally mocked. 'You're virtually impossible to work with, let alone be with twenty-four hours a day.'

'I take it this is what friends are for?' he rasped. 'To insult you?'

'To tell you the truth when necessary, sweetie,' she touched his cheek affectionately.

'Well, today I can do without it,' he dismissed

harshly. 'Come through to the studio if you want to talk to me, if you don't then stop keeping my employees from their work,' he added coldly.

Lindsay was still pale from his last dig at her. This last one made her flinch, something Joel seemed as immune to as he was every other emotion. She didn't know how she could ever have fooled herself into thinking he would one day love her!

'Here's the file you wanted.' She handed it to him, taking care not to touch him, a fact he seemed well aware of as his mouth twisted derisively.

He nodded acknowledgement of the file, turning to Cally. 'Are you staying or going?'

'Much as I hate to turn down your gracious invitation,' she mocked him, her eyes gleaming with mischief, 'I have to meet David in a few minutes, so I can't stay long. I actually came round to invite you both to dinner at the weekend. Although in the circumstances perhaps I should say invite you both *and* your respective partners.' She looked at them with feigned innocence.

Joel's scowl deepened, and Lindsay wondered, not for the first time, how Cally dared to antagonise him when he was in this mood. She always steered clear of him at such times, although perhaps Cally felt that their past association allowed her to goad him in this way.

'Suits me,' he snapped. 'Just tell me what time and day, and I'll be there.'

'Saturday, eight o'clock.' She looked enquiringly at Lindsay. 'Is that okay for you?'

Any evening and time suited her at the moment, they were all free. But she had no idea who she could take as her 'partner' for the evening. 'Fine,' she agreed lightly, ignoring the way Joel's eyes narrowed speculatively. No doubt he would have no trouble at all finding someone to accompany him!

'Now, Joel,' Cally put her arm through the crook of his arm, walking into the studio with him, 'I just have time for you to tell me all about . . .'

The rest of the conversation was cut off as Joel firmly closed the door behind them. Lindsay put up a shaking hand to her temple, as she sat down behind her desk. The next month, while she worked her notice, was going to seem a very long time indeed.

'Hey, are you all right?' asked a concerned voice, the accent distinctly American. 'You look a little pale.'

Lindsay looked up into the attractive face of the man leaning over her desk, a man of about forty, possibly a little younger, with dark hair heavily tinged with grey at his temples, and pale blue eyes that could also look grey in certain lights or moods. Even leaning over as he was she could see he was tall, his tailored suit fitting him well, his lean body containing a liquid grace that spoke of training of movement.

'I'm fine.' She sat up straighter in her chair, a little unnerved by the way he kept staring at her with warm blue eyes. 'And I'm afraid the agency who sent you must have made a mistake—Mr Sutherland doesn't photograph male models.'

The man looked amused by the assumption, and straightened slightly, the blue eyes twinkling merrily. 'I'm flattered you should think me young enough or attractive enough to be a male model,' he drawled softly. 'But isn't forty-one a little old for all that?' He raised dark brows.

'It really depends what line of modelling you're interested in,' she shrugged.

'I really shouldn't be teasing you in this way,' he smiled, laughter lines fanning out from his eyes in the tanned face. 'Malcolm Reader,' and he put out his hand in friendly greeting.

Lindsay gave a start of surprise. *This* was the famous Malcolm Reader, the man who had made millions in the cosmetic business? He didn't seem old enough or ruthless enough, although she sensed a certain steel in his nature beneath the easy charm. But she hadn't realised he was in England. Did Jöel?

'Lindsay Pope.' She put her hand into his, finding it lost in his much bigger grip, his hand surprisingly firm and calloused considering he must spend most of his time seated behind a desk.

'Rope burn,' he seemed to guess her thoughts. 'I spend most of my weekends sailing. And I know exactly who you are, Joel spoke of you often when he was in New York.'

'Oh yes?' she asked warily, aware that he had forgotten to release her hand, and extricating it herself.

Blue eyes looked at her steadily. 'Yes.'

Delicate colour darkened her cheeks. 'I can't imagine what he said,' she evaded.

'Can't you?'

'No!'

'Well, he didn't tell me how beautiful you are, for one thing,' his teasing manner was back. 'You wouldn't take pity on a visitor to London and have dinner with me one evening, would you?' He looked at her encouragingly.

'I——'

'Malcolm!' Joel greeted harshly behind them, looking accusingly at Lindsay. 'Why didn't you tell me Mr Reader was here?' he rasped.

'I've only just arrived,' the other man exaggerated, moving forward to shake his outstretched hand. 'Your secretary was taking very good care of me. And who is this beautiful young lady?' He looked appreciatively at Cally.

Lindsay took the opportunity while they made the introductions of fading into the background. Whatever Joel had told the other man about her he couldn't have told him they were living together, Malcolm Reader would hardly have been likely to invite her out if he had! She felt grateful for the fact that she hadn't had to make any reply to his invitation, not wanting to upset a man who was so important to Joel, but still feeling too raw from her break-up with Joel to contemplate seeing another man.

'Handsome devil,' Cally remarked thoughtfully, the two men being ensconced in the inner office now. 'He's worth cultivating, Lindsay,' she added softly.

'Whatever do you mean by cultivate, Cally?' asked Lindsay, tongue-in-cheek.

Deep blue eyes glowed with amusement. 'You know very well what I mean. And he was attracted to you too, I could tell.'

'Really?' she said uninterestedly. Tall, dark, handsome men were not on her list of favourite things at the moment.

'Really,' Cally insisted forcefully. 'Has it ever occurred to you that all Joel needs is a little old-fashioned jealousy to make him realise what he's giving up?'

'He doesn't even know the meaning of the word,' Lindsay dismissed with bitterness.

'Don't you believe it,' the other woman said with certainty. 'Just because he doesn't show it it doesn't mean he doesn't feel it. He's just adept at hiding what he really feels.'

Lindsay sighed. 'I know you mean well, Cally,' she

said softly. 'But it's over between Joel and me. I think six months is long enough for anyone to realise they're banging their head rather painfully against a brick wall. Right now I just want to get my life back in order, and then get on with it. And none of that involves Joel.'

'I see,' Cally sighed with regret. 'It's a shame—I really thought that with you he was getting it all together. He's seemed more relaxed since you lived with him, less inclined to retreat inside his emotions. Still, if you say it's over then it's over,' she shrugged.

'It is,' Lindsay nodded. 'I've also given in my notice today.'

'So he told me. Well, I'll see you Saturday, then?' Cally quirked auburn brows.

'I'm not sure——'

'Oh, you have to come,' the other woman encouraged. 'Joel is sure to, and if you don't turn up he'll know it was because you couldn't face him on a social level.'

'I don't think I can,' Lindsay admitted huskily.

'Of course you can,' Cally told her firmly. 'And bring along some handsome man just to prove it.'

Lindsay's mouth twisted. 'I don't know any handsome men.'

'What about Malcolm Reader?'

That idea had fleetingly entered her own mind, but she had as quickly dismissed it. He was a pleasant enough man, seemed very nice, was undoubtedly handsome, but he was also a very important client of Joel's, convincing her that she shouldn't become involved with him on a social level. Joel would certainly never forgive her if she upset the other man in any way!

'He's business,' she shrugged. 'So he doesn't count.'

'He looked as if he counted to me,' Cally teased.

'He's probably married with half a dozen children!'

Cally shook her head. 'He's one of America's most eligible bachelors.'

'Then what is his problem?' Lindsay frowned.

The other woman laughed. 'He doesn't have one, except maybe that he just hasn't met the right woman yet. You could be her, Lindsay. Just think what a blow that would be to Joel's pride!'

'I'm not out to hurt anyone, Cally,' Lindsay said wearily. 'I just want to forget any of this ever happened.'

'Do you think you can?'

'No.'

'I'm beginning to feel guilty because I'm so happy,' Cally grimaced, kissing Lindsay on the cheek by way of departure. 'You'll never get over the selfish swine completely,' she said huskily. 'But once the love stops being so intense it doesn't hurt so much. Take my word for it,' she added ruefully.

Lindsay had always suspected the other woman's feelings had been more deeply involved with Joel in the past than she had admitted to, and Cally had just confirmed it. But Cally had had four years to get over her love for him, while she only had as many days if she were to go to the other woman's dinner party on Saturday and see him with another woman with any degree of confidence. The way her heart ached at the moment she didn't think she was going to make it.

'I'll try,' she nodded. 'And I'll call you about Saturday,' she promised.

'I really would like you to come,' Cally encouraged before leaving to meet her husband.

Lindsay was engrossed in her work when Malcolm Reader left Joel's studio an hour later, the older man coming over to talk to her as Joel took into his studio the model that had been waiting outside to begin her session with him.

'Nice life if you can get it,' Malcolm Reader mocked lightly, sitting on the edge of Lindsay's desk.

'I've heard that you have,' she said dryly, looking up at him guilelessly.

He chuckled softly. 'The beautiful Mrs Robin has heard of my reputation, hmm?'

Lindsay nodded. 'And all of it exaggerated, no doubt,' she mocked.

'Very little, I'm afraid,' he drawled derisively.

She had to laugh at his honesty, feeling humour when a few minutes ago she had thought she would never laugh again. 'That's interesting to know,' she smiled.

'Only interesting?' He looked disappointed. 'Most women are eager to find out the truth for themselves.'

'I'll be happy to take your word for it,' she teased lightly, liking this man in spite of his outrageous sense of humour.

'Pity,' he drawled. 'Did you give some thought to my dinner invitation?' He quirked dark brows. 'As I recall you hadn't answered me when we were interrupted.'

Her amusement instantly faded. 'It's very nice of you to ask me, Mr Reader——'

'When a beautiful woman calls me "Mr" then I know I'm going to be turned down!' he grinned ruefully. 'And I was hoping you would show me the highlights of London.'

'I don't know that many,' she shrugged. 'And I'm sure you've been to London before?'

'Many times,' he nodded. 'It's a fascinating place.'

'Surely no more so than New York?'

'In a different way,' he replied thoughtfully. 'And I find most of my enjoyment of London by seeing it through the eyes of other people.'

'Women's eyes,' she teased.

'Women's eyes,' he confirmed with a smile. 'Have you ever been to New York?'

Lindsay shook her head. 'I've never been out of England.'

'Joel should have brought you with him, I would have enjoyed showing you my home town.'

If she had been invited by Joel to go on his business trip maybe she wouldn't have left him. But although their last night together had been spent in a frenzy of lovemaking Joel hadn't once suggested she accompany him. 'Someone had to run the office while he was away,' she said with forced brightness.

'I guess so,' Malcolm Reader conceded. 'Although it seems a pity we couldn't have met earlier.'

If they had met before he would now know her to be Joel's ex-mistress. The two of them had never broadcast their living arrangements, but they had made no secret of it either, admitting it if asked directly. If they had gone to New York together then Malcolm Reader would know exactly what she was. And somehow she didn't want him to know.

'Is there already a man in your life?' Malcom was asking her now.

Lindsay looked up with a start, having been lost in thought. 'Sorry?'

'Am I stepping on some lucky man's toes by making the dinner invitation?' he explained.

'No!' She blushed as she realised how sharply her denial had come out, almost guiltily. 'No, it isn't that,' she said more calmly. 'It's just——'

'It's okay, Lindsay,' he chuckled as he stood up. 'I

can take no for an answer without putting you on the rack. I just wanted to make sure I wasn't making an absolute idiot of myself if I kept asking. And I will keep asking, Lindsay,' he added seriously. 'You'll find I'm not a man who gives up easily.'

'That's okay,' her own voice was light, 'because I don't give in easily either.'

He smiled his appreciation of her show of independence, little knowing that she was all the more determined not to be charmed by him because she had so recently been hurt by a man with even less charm than him. 'Good girl,' he straightened. 'But I'll be seeing you soon.'

It was a promise, not a threat, and Lindsay was left with the feeling that Malcolm Reader was a man with as much strength of will as Joel, that he wouldn't give up easily either, although perhaps his method of getting his own way would be more subtle than Joel's. But Cally had been right about one thing—Malcolm Reader certainly didn't have a problem!

'Planning to replace me already?' Joel rasped harshly.

Lindsay looked up at him coolly, although her heart rate accelerated considerably, having been unaware of the model leaving and Joel watching her. 'Hardly,' she drawled. 'Although Mr Reader seems a very charming man,' she added challengingly.

'Oh, he is,' Joel scorned. 'Maybe he could even charm you into living with him. But if you think I'm a bastard you should—God, I'm sorry,' he groaned as he saw her pale. 'I didn't mean it that way. Lindsay? Lindsay——!' he questioned sharply as she suddenly stood up to collect her jacket and handbag.

'I'm going to lunch,' she told him stiffly. 'I know it's a little earlier than my usual time, but I—I feel as if I need the break now. I'll be back in an hour,' she added firmly as she heard her voice begin to quiver with emotion.

'Lindsay——'

'An hour, Joel.' She couldn't even look at him as she rushed from the office and out of the building, not looking back once as she hurried down the street, not even sure where she was going, just needing to get away, away from Joel and his power to hurt her with every word he spoke.

Never before had Joel chosen to hurt her the way he was doing at the moment, seeming to hit out at her on purpose, something he had never done before today. Oh, he had a temper, a whiplash tongue at times, but his remarks had never been personal before; never designed to hurt and go on hurting.

She didn't stop walking for the next hour, although she never afterwards knew where she went, only that she walked and walked, sightlessly pushing Joel to the back of her mind.

But finally she had to think of him, of facing him again, and if he was still in that cruelly hurtful mood when she did, when he could taunt the way she had loved him enough to move in with him, she didn't know what she would do.

He was sitting at her desk when she got back, watching her warily as she woodenly hung up her jacket and smoothed her hair. 'I'm sorry,' he finally spoke, his voice husky. 'I didn't mean that remark about Reader.' His eyes were a stormy tawny gold as he looked at her searchingly. 'Do you believe me?' he prompted at her continued silence.

'Of course,' she acknowledged flatly.

He stood up, coming round to the front of her desk, the warmth of his body reaching out to her in the confines of the room. 'He did ask you out, though, didn't he?' his eyes narrowed.

She looked at him unflinchingly. 'And if he did?'

Joel's hands clenched into fists at his sides. 'I could tell he was attracted to you,' he ground out.

'If I didn't know you better, Joel,' she taunted, 'and luckily I do,' she added hardly, 'I would think you cared.'

His mouth tightened. 'I care that because of the way we've parted you might find yourself involved when you don't really want to be.'

Lindsay looked at him with dislike. 'And since when did you become an expert on what I want?' She knew it was the wrong thing to say even as she said it, the soft colour flooding her cheeks. Joel knew exactly what she wanted, what she needed, when it came to making love! His eyes mocked her with that knowledge now. 'I meant emotionally,' she snapped.

He ignored the jibe. 'Are you going out with Reader?' he persisted in the subject of the other man.

Lindsay shrugged. 'I might. But I doubt it,' she added as his eyes darkened stormily. 'I've learnt the hard way that mixing business and pleasure just doesn't work out.'

His mouth tightened. 'Which part of that applies to your relationship with me the last six months?'

She swallowed hard. 'I'm beginning to think neither!'

Joel gave a deep sigh, closing his eyes momentarily. 'God, I can't seem to stop hitting out at you. Maybe you're right to want to leave, after all,' he shook his head. 'I'm only hurting you.'

'You have to care to be hurt,' she sat down behind her desk, paler than ever, 'and we've agreed that neither of us does that.'

'Yes,' he bit out. 'I think I'll go to lunch now,' he added suddenly, leaving abruptly.

Lindsay's shattered nerves relaxed slowly once he had left. This was so much more traumatic than even she had imagined, Joel reacting much more strongly than she had thought he would. She had seen the women come and go in his life for so long, and he had never been so bitter about it before. But then it had never been the woman's decision to end things before. Joel seemed to have an inborn radar that warned him when a woman was becoming too emotionally involved with him, and at the first sign of that he would end things between them, usually with a bouquet of flowers and a carefully worded note. Maybe if she didn't love him so much she would have sent *him* flowers and a carefully worded note!

The uneasy truce that existed between them over the next few days made the studio hell to go to, but Lindsay was determined not to show any sign of weakness by not going in. Joel had shown her all too clearly when she had almost admitted her love for him how much he deplored such human frailties.

But the strain showed on her as the week progressed, her days fraught with tension as Joel remained likely to explode at the slightest provocation, her nights no easier as she ached for his arms about her, his body filling her as they cried out their enjoyment of each other.

The tension between them wasn't helped by the fact that Malcolm Reader was likely to call in or telephone her without warning. As promised, he hadn't given up asking her to go out with him, and he was proving to be as persistent as Joel had once been. Malcolm's frequent presence in his secretary's office was viewed with anger by Joel, and she felt sure it was only that he was working for Malcolm that kept him from asking the other man to leave.

Joel returned the file of the models he had used during the last five years on Thursday lunchtime, his sigh one of dissatisfaction.

'No luck?' She looked up at him with a frown, knowing there were some really beautiful women in there.

'No,' he rasped.

'But surely one of them is suitable?'

'Suitable, yes,' he bit out. 'But I happen to want someone who's perfect.'

If the strain of the last four days showed on her then Joel hadn't escaped unscathed either. Of course he was going out every night, usually with a different woman, and apparently not getting in until the early hours of the morning, when undoubtedly he didn't sleep alone. He certainly looked tired, with lines beside his eyes, the sharp sense of humour he had once possessed no longer in evidence. Even if he were now making up for lost time with an abundance of different women he certainly didn't look happy about it.

But Lindsay felt no satisfaction from knowing that, knew such deep unhappiness herself that if Joel felt even one tenth of the misery she did then she pitied him.

'Perhaps you're being too critical, Joel,' she reasoned. 'After all, the make-up is surely meant for a number of different women, not just one type.'

He shook his head. 'It's an exclusive line, meant only for brunettes.'

'But you've photographed hundreds of brunettes——'

'None of them are suitable for what I want for this,' he insisted harshly.

She could see he felt very deeply about the model he used. If there was one thing Joel did feel passion and fire for it was his work. 'What is it you want, Joel?' she prompted softly.

His eyes hardened. 'A black-haired, green-eyed witch,' he spoke with quiet vehemence, as if the thought didn't please him at all. 'The name of the new line is "Witchcraft",' he explained.

Lindsay chewed on her bottom lip. 'I see.'

'I doubt it,' he dismissed scornfully. 'You have no idea what it's like to have a vision and know only that vision will do!'

She stiffened. 'I have dreams too, Joel,' she told him curtly.

'This isn't a dream,' he rasped harshly, his face set in cold lines. 'This is a reality, *she's* a reality. A reality that haunts me day and night!'

'Joel . . .?'

He looked at her as if he were seeing her for the first time, his eyes becoming emotionless as he realised how much he had revealed. 'Forget it,' he said curtly. 'It isn't important.'

It was obviously very important to him, this woman who still had the power to hurt and disturb him. Lindsay hadn't thought there could ever be such a woman. 'Joel——'

'I said forget it!' His fierce harshness had the effect of silencing her. 'There has to be someone else I can use for this advertising,' he spoke almost to himself. 'I refuse to even think about using her.'

'Why?' she prompted, knowing he must have already thought about using this mystery woman.

His eyes flared deeply tawny. 'Mind your own

damned business!' His face twisted angrily.

Lindsay flinched at this show of aggression, feeling pain that it was another woman who was causing him such torment. It seemed he hadn't always been as insensitive to the emotion love as he was now, that a woman had once, painfully, shown him its exact meaning.

'Just stay the hell out of my life!' Joel told her savagely before slamming out of the office.

She had never seen him so upset, and she wondered who the woman could be who had once hurt him so much. She had known there had to be a reason for his derision of love, but had hoped it had something to do with the way he never talked about his parents, that perhaps an unhappy childhood had tainted the idea of love and marriage for him. It hurt to know that all the time she had been hoping for him to fall in love with her she had been fighting the memory of another woman he just couldn't forget.

When he returned to the office a couple of hours later he was more subdued than Lindsay had ever seen him, a dull acceptance in his eyes. Her heart ached for the fact that he had never been able to share his pain.

He stopped in front of her desk. 'Somewhere in the files you'll find one on Marilyn Mills. Bring it in to me as soon as you find it.'

Marilyn Mills. So she even had a name for the woman now. And whatever had happened to separate Joel and the other woman in the past, he had obviously decided to see her now.

She had some difficulty finding the folder, finally locating it buried at the back of one of the older filing cabinets. But as soon as she opened it and saw the top photograph of the beautiful woman she knew the reason for Joel's torment. Marilyn Mills was indeed a black-haired, green-eyed witch, an exquisitely beautiful one!

CHAPTER THREE

'I ASKED you to bring it in as soon as you found it,' Joel bit out tautly.

Lindsay met his gaze reluctantly, knowing she was guilty of prying, something he wouldn't tolerate. If only he didn't move so stealthily, she might occasionally have warning of his impending presence! 'I was just checking that I had the right Marilyn Mills,' she invented lamely.

The mockery in his eyes said he knew she lied. 'Believe me,' he scowled, 'there's only one.'

She moistened her lips nervously. 'Isn't she a little old now? After all, you used her seven years ago.'

'You have been busy, haven't you?' he drawled hardly. 'And I wouldn't call twenty-five old.'

Lindsay's eyes widened. 'She was only eighteen when these photographs were taken?'

'Yes.' His mouth twisted with bitterness. 'Hard to believe, isn't it?'

Difficult to imagine, was more like it. The woman in the beautifully alluring photographs looked as if she had never been anything *less* than a woman; there was not even a hint of innocence in the provocative green eyes.

'She's very lovely,' Lindsay told him woodenly.

'Very,' he acknowledged abruptly, picking up the folder containing the photographs.

Lindsay felt a knife twist in her chest. 'Why haven't you used her for seven years?' she asked recklessly.

He looked positively violent. 'She stopped modelling for a while,' he revealed through gritted teeth.

'And now?' she prompted.

'Now she lives and works in the States.' His eyes flickered over her coolly. 'Why all the interest, Lindsay?'

She shrugged. 'As I said, she's beautiful——'

'All my models are beautiful,' he dismissed that excuse.

Her eyes flashed deeply green as she looked up at him. 'Not all of them affect you in this way.'

Joel stiffened, white tension about his mouth. 'What way?' he asked tautly.

Lindsay moistened her lips, realising that perhaps she had gone too far. Joel had always rebuffed any intrusion into his past or private life, and he was hardly likely to welcome her interest in his past love. 'Forget I said it,' she told him briskly. 'I have some letters here that need your signature——'

'In what way, Lindsay?' he persisted harshly, grasping her arm painfully.

'Joel, you're hurting me!' she choked in a surprised voice, never having known him to be physically violent with her before. He had never had any need to be, not when physical seduction could be so much more enjoyable—for both of them.

'Tell me, damn you!'

She swallowed hard, knowing he wasn't going to let her go until he had his answer. 'In this way,' she told him shakily. 'I've never seen you enjoy hurting someone before.'

'Damn!' he swore with impatience, pushing her away from him as if she burnt him, thrusting his hands into the pockets of his dark trousers, the jacket to his suit discarded in the studio, his light blue shirt stretched tautly across his chest. 'Why do I always find myself apologising to you lately?' He looked at her with troubled eyes. 'Have you found your replacement yet?' he continued without waiting for an answer.

Lindsay resisted the impulse she had to rub the area of her arm that throbbed beneath her black silky blouse. 'I thought you would want to do that,' she mumbled, looking down at her desk.

'I don't,' he dismissed coldly. 'Find her and train her. I don't want to be bothered with it.'

Lindsay blinked back the tears. 'Very well.'

'Have you found another job yourself yet?' He lingered in the room.

She hadn't even looked! And she would have to if she wanted to continue paying the rent on her flat and not face the added humiliation of going home to live at her mother's house. That was something she just couldn't bear; relations between her mother and herself were still very strained the last time she had telephoned home.

'Not yet,' she told him brightly. 'But I'm confident I'll find something.'

His eyes were glacial. 'Roger's still looking for someone,' he revealed with reluctance.

'I don't think so,' she refused softly. 'I think I'll look for something a little more—routine.'

His mouth twisted. 'You would be bored with that within a week!'

Lindsay looked up at him unflinchingly. 'Maybe boredom is what I want.'

Joel looked as if she had physically hit him. 'I'm glad I gave you some excitement in your life for a few months,' he rasped.

She sighed. 'You're deliberately misunderstanding me.'

'Am I?' he scowled. 'I don't——' he broke off as the telephone began to ring. 'You'd better answer that, I'd hate you to miss any of Reader's calls,' he added derisively.

'So would I,' she was goaded into retorting, as she picked up the receiver. 'Joel Sutherland's studio,' she recited automatically.

'It's Cally, Lindsay,' came the instant cheerful response. 'You promised you would call me about Saturday, and you haven't,' she admonished.

'Saturday?' Lindsay echoed, looking up at Joel as he muttered something, putting her hand over the mouthpiece. 'What did you say?' she frowned.

'I said I'll leave you to your call,' he said harshly.

'Joel——' Too late; he had already gone through to the studio, the scowl on his face telling her that he wasn't pleased at the thought of Malcolm calling her here. Not that that meant he had to feel anything personal about it, he could just object as her employer; she shouldn't be receiving personal calls at the office.

'Am I interrupting something?' Cally asked interestedly.

'Not a thing.' Lindsay turned her attention to the other woman. 'I'm sorry about Saturday——'

'You've decided not to come.' Cally couldn't hide her disappointment.

'No, I didn't mean that,' Lindsay laughed lightly. 'I'm sorry I didn't get back to you about it. I do have someone I can bring with me——'

'Malcolm Reader?'

'No,' she derided with amusement. 'My sister is coming to stay with me for the weekend, and I thought——'

'Your *sister*?' Cally groaned her dismay. 'I thought you meant a *male* companion.'

'Does that mean I can't bring Judi?' she teased.

'Of course not,' the other woman sighed. 'Although it will put my seating arrangements out.'

'I'm sure you'll cope.'

'I'm sure I will too,' Cally laughed. 'Although I could have sworn Malcolm Reader was attracted to you.'

'Who said he isn't?'

'And you've turned him down?' the other woman groaned her incredulity. 'Lindsay, I despair of you! The man has everything, looks, charm, money, and not least of all, sex appeal.'

She was well aware of all that, and at any other time she might have been attracted to him in return. But not now, not when the only man she could still see or hear was Joel.

As if guessing some of her thoughts Cally spoke of him. 'Joel is coming—and I doubt he'll bring along his brother!' she added derisively.

'He doesn't have one,' said Lindsay dryly.

'He did,' Cally told her seriously. 'As I understand it, he died years ago.'

Once again Lindsay was made aware of how little Joel had ever confided in her. He could have ten brothers *and* sisters for all she knew! 'As you say, I doubt he'll bring anything but a beautiful woman,' she said bitterly.

'Lindsay——'

'I have to go now, Cally,' she cut in hastily, knowing the other woman meant well, but still not up to any tête-à-tête chats for the moment. 'I'll see you Saturday evening.'

She had been pleased when Judi asked if she could come and stay this weekend, welcoming her sister's company during a weekend that stretched out in front of her like a black void. Maybe Judi had understood that and that was the reason she had decided on the visit. Whatever the reason, Lindsay was grateful.

Joel didn't mention the telephone call or the folder on Marilyn Mills when she saw him next, and Lindsay warily steered clear of any subject that might prove inflammatory as it had that morning.

But she was relieved when Friday came around, knowing that she needed the two days' respite from walking on a razor's edge, although Saturday evening wasn't something she was looking forward to. Not that Joel gave any indication of flaring up at her as he had yesterday; he was in quite a good mood as he slapped the Marilyn Mills file back down on her desk and went to lunch.

Lindsay had no idea what he wanted her to do with the folder, and carefully placed it to one side of her desk, curious to look through it again and yet remembering what had happened last time she did. It would be just like Joel to come back unexpectedly and catch her in the act

She almost fell off her chair when the outside door did open, her hand guiltily leaving the Marilyn Mills folder as she was tempted to open it, her relief immense when she saw Malcolm entering her office, her smile bright as she looked at him.

'What did I do to deserve that?' He strolled over lazily, as handsome as ever in fitted blue trousers and a navy blue shirt, his eyes a deep blue today as he removed his sunglasses, slipping them into the breast pocket of his shirt.

'You aren't Joel.' She was too relieved to see him to prevaricate.

'You noticed,' he grinned, sitting at his usual place on the edge of her desk.

'Yes, I noticed,' she derided.

'I wondered,' he said ruefully. 'Only you treat me with the same wariness you treat him,' he explained at her questioning look.

Delicate colour highlighted her cheeks. 'I'm sure you're mistaken. Joel is my boss, I naturally treat him with a certain amount of respect and——'

'Wariness,' Malcolm finished firmly. 'What's he done, chased you around the office a few times?'

She stiffened. 'That's hardly Joel's style.'

'I couldn't blame him if he had,' he shrugged. 'I'd be tempted to myself.'

'Well, he hasn't,' she said waspishly. 'Now what can I do for you? Joel is at lunch, I'm afraid——'

'You know I didn't come here to see Joel,' Malcolm drawled dismissively. 'I thought *we* might have lunch.'

'I've already eaten, thank you,' Lindsay answered abruptly, wishing he would take the hint and stop asking her out; she was running out of politeness where he was concerned.

He looked chagrined. 'Why is that always the case?'

'Maybe if you telephoned first. . . .'

'I would still get absolutely nowhere,' he said shrewdly. 'I've come to the conclusion that you really aren't interested in going out with me.'

Now she felt guilty. 'It's nothing personal, I can assure you. I just——'

'He hurt you pretty badly, didn't he,' Malcolm frowned.

She looked up at him sharply. 'He?'

'Hey, what's this?' He had accidentally knocked against the Marilyn Mills folder, and several of the loose photographs fell out over Lindsay's desk. 'She's beautiful.' He picked up the top photograph, whistling softly through his teeth. 'Who is she?' he asked with narrowed eyes.

Lindsay was glad to have the subject changed from her own personal life, although Malcolm's interest in the lovely model might not be something Joel wanted. 'Just a model.' She put her hand out for the photograph.

Malcolm ignored her outstretched hand, picking up yet more of the photographs. 'She isn't *just* anything, Lindsay, she's fantastic,' he said slowly.

She had to agree with him, but she still wasn't sure how Joel was going to feel about this.

Malcolm looked up questioningly. 'I hope Joel has signed her up to do my advertising?'

Lindsay avoided his gaze. 'He wouldn't consider anyone without discussing it with you first.' That much, at least, was true!

'This girl is perfect for what I want,' said Malcolm with bubbling eagerness.

'She's hardly a girl now,' Lindsay told him abruptly. 'Those photographs are several years old.'

'I don't care how old they are.' His enthusiasm couldn't be denied. 'I have to have her!'

Lindsay's eyes widened at his forcefulness. 'I'm afraid that's for you and Joel to discuss,' and she carefully placed all the photographs back in the folder, closing it firmly.

'There's nothing to discuss,' Malcolm decided arrogantly. 'I've found my "Witchcraft" girl. You can tell Joel that when he gets back.' He stood up.

She grimaced at the thought. 'I'd much rather *you* told him.'

He looked at her questioningly, finally nodding ruefully. 'Maybe you're right at that—I did pry into private documents on your desk. Joel isn't going to be too pleased about that, hm?'

That had to be the understatement of the year; Joel wasn't going to like it at all! 'You could say that!' Her expression was rueful.

'Oh, I do,' he said with amusement. 'Now what were we talking about before I saw that exquisitely beautiful woman?'

Lindsay avoided his eyes. 'You'd just decided to accept the fact that I won't go out with you, and were in the process of leaving.'

'In other words, I was prying into something that was none of my business,' he realised dryly.

'In other words,' she nodded stiffly.

He shrugged. 'I'll come back later and talk to Joel. I wish I knew where I went wrong with you,' he added thoughtfully.

She smiled. 'You didn't go wrong, Malcolm, it was just bad timing, that's all.'

'That recent, hm?'

'Yes,' she confirmed abruptly.

He sighed. 'That's a pity, I would have liked to get to know you better.'

'What I am is what you see,' she smiled again.

'And what I see is a warm, beautiful woman.' He shrugged his regret. 'I'm just sorry I was too late.'

'Or too soon.'

He shook his head slowly. 'I have a feeling that with you it will always be too late—whoever he is, he's made a lasting impression on you.'

Lindsay's deep unhappiness was reflected in the smoky green of her eyes. 'Thank you for understanding.'

He touched her hand briefly. 'I don't understand, I accept. I'll just have to find some other poor woman to badger,' he smiled. 'Now I suppose I'd better let you get back to work. But I'll be back to see Joel later,' he warned again, showing her that he had far from forgotten the subject of Marilyn Mills.

And that was what she was afraid of. Joel might have already accepted that he was going to use the glamorous model for this assignment, she just didn't know; what she did know was that he wouldn't like the decision being taken out of his hands. And the way Malcolm was talking he didn't intend to give Joel any choice in the matter.

Joel was in his studio when Malcolm returned later that afternoon, and it was with some misgivings that she told him the other man was here to see him, asking Malcolm to wait while Joel finished his photographic session.

'Did you mention to him what I want to see him about?' Malcolm asked curiously.

'No.'

'Afraid to?' he teased.

'Yes,' she answered without prevarication.

Malcolm grinned. 'Has he always been this rough to work with?'

'Not always, no.'

'No?' His brows rose interestedly. 'What's happened to make him into such a taskmaster?'

Lindsay was saved the embarrassment of having to answer by Joel appearing to invite the other man through to the studio.

She couldn't hear the sound of raised voices from the adjoining room as she made an effort to look as if she were working, too keyed up about this meeting to really concentrate. She had no doubt about Joel's reaction to being manipulated in this way, just as she had no doubt who would get the blame for it. It was enough to make her want to turn tail and run for cover!

But she didn't, knowing that if Joel was angry enough he would seek her out and have his say. Much better to stay and face him here.

Malcolm looked very pleased with himself when he emerged forty minutes later, smiling triumphantly at Lindsay. 'Not a scratch on me!' he taunted.

Her brows rose. 'Did you expect there to be?'

'From the way you've been acting, yes!'

She shrugged lightly. 'You never can tell how Joel will react to these things.'

'He was the perfect gentleman,' Malcolm assured her with satisfaction.

She doubted the other man would look so pleased with himself if he knew that was the time Joel was at his most dangerous! Although she doubted he would ever direct his anger at this man, and that made her position as scapegoat all the more precarious. 'Well I'm glad it went well for you,' she said noncommittally.

'Ah, now, I didn't say that, did I?' he grimaced ruefully.

'You mean it didn't go well?'

'He's thinking about the idea,' Malcolm admitted somewhat reluctantly; obviously he was not a man who liked—or even had—his wishes *thought* about.

Lindsay could well imagine the clash of wills that had gone on in the other room, albeit politely, both men being determined to have their own way. Maybe it would have been worth witnessing, after all! 'I'm sure Joel will do what you want him to,' she said soothingly.

'Are you?' He pulled a face. 'I'm not so sure. But I refuse to use anyone else for my advertising campaign. I want Marilyn Mills up on posters fifty foot high!'

That he also found the other woman extremely

fascinating and desirable was obvious. 'There's always the possibility that Miss Mills no longer models,' she pointed out practically.

'That's up to Joel to find out,' he reminded her with arrogance. 'If she doesn't then I'm sure we can exert sufficient incentive to entice her back into the business.'

Lindsay looked at him with wide-eyed admiration. 'You really are ruthless, aren't you?'

He grinned a disarmingly boyish smile. 'You'd better believe it!'

She did. Joel must have met his match today, and he wasn't going to like it. She eyed the adjoining door with trepidation, the fact that Joel hadn't already come bursting through it adding to her sense of unease. His flares of violently verbal temper were easy to deal with, she usually just sat quietly until the storm had passed, but when things were quiet and calm she knew to expect real trouble; Joel was furious!

She looked up as he came through ten minutes later, his face set in uncompromising lines, his eyes dark tawny. 'Joel——' she began tentatively.

He looked at her coldly. 'You may as well leave for the weekend if you're finished there.'

She swallowed hard. 'Joel——'

'And if you feel you are no longer capable of being my *confidential* secretary then just say so and we can terminate this arrangement right here and now.' He looked at her with icy challenge.

Lindsay gasped her dismay. 'Joel, I couldn't help Malcolm seeing that file——'

'Couldn't you?' he scorned harshly. 'Oh, I think you knew exactly what you were doing!'

'No!'

'Yes!' he hissed vehemently, deep lines grooved into

his face as the coldness broke into red-hot anger. 'I think you're enjoying this.'

She was very pale, even the fact that she had expected his anger not preparing her for this. 'I couldn't stop Malcolm looking at the folder,' she defended. 'It was on top of my desk, and——'

'So you showed it to him!'

'No, of course not!'

'Then you were so engrossed in his charm that you forgot your loyalty to *me* and let him see it!' Joel accused with rigid anger.

'No——'

'Do you think the fact that we once lived together gives you the right to interfere like this?' he continued remorselessly, glaring at her with fierce dislike.

He made it sound as if that 'living together' had taken place years ago rather than just a week! 'I'm well aware of the fact that our once living together gives me no rights where you're concerned,' she choked. 'It never did!'

'As long as you understand that,' he bit out coldly, bending over her desk threateningly. 'Because I won't tolerate this interference in my life.'

'You aren't going to use Marilyn Mills?' Her voice quivered softly.

'I'll use who I damn well please,' he rasped. 'If Marilyn pleases me then I'll use her, if not then I won't. I won't be dictated to by anyone! Do you understand?'

Lindsay understood that Joel's anger against her was making him irresponsible to his career, that he was forgetting he was an employee too at the moment, just as she was. 'Malcolm is your client——'

'And clients can be dropped——'

'Joel, he's an important man——'

'I don't give a damn who or what he is,' he rasped. 'Everyone is expendable in this world.'

'Even you,' she said softly.

'Even me,' he nodded tautly. 'I'm not forcing Reader to stay with me.'

'But if you get the reputation of being temperamental——'

'I'm sure I already have one,' his mouth twisted with derision. 'It doesn't stop the work pouring in.'

Lindsay tried one last time to reason with him, knowing that his anger was making him reckless—and cruelly hurtful. She was well aware that the comment about everyone being expendable was directed at her as much as Malcolm Reader. 'Joel, you can't upset an important client like him——'

'Watch me!' he ground out.

'Would it be so bad to use Marilyn Mills?' she persisted gently.

'Yes, it would be bad.' He was breathing heavily in his agitation. 'You don't know how bad!'

She felt inward pain that the other woman could still hurt him so badly. 'Would you like to talk to me about her——'

'No!' He moved back as if she burnt him. 'Don't try and psychoanalyse me, Lindsay,' he added tauntingly. 'The part of my life that once involved Marilyn is a closed book to you and everyone else. Understood?'

'Understood,' she nodded, blinking back the tears so that he shouldn't see them.

'As long as it is,' he grated.

'Do you still want me to leave your employment today?' she halted him at the door.

He turned slowly. 'That's entirely up to you.' He looked at her emotionlessly. 'How does your confidentiality stand?'

'The way that it's always stood,' she told him between stiff lips. 'With you.'

'Then there's no problem, is there?' he shrugged dismissively, as if he hadn't just hurt her unbearably.

'I wish you would just let me explain how Malcolm came to see that folder——'

'I don't want you to explain anything about Malcolm to me,' he told her abruptly. 'Just make sure your relationship with him stays out of my studio in future.'

'I don't have a relationship with him,' she protested. 'I like him, but I'm not going out with him.'

'It's really none of my business what you do in your own time,' Joel dismissed uninterestedly.

'No,' she acknowledged softly. 'What do you want me to do about Miss Mills?'

'I don't want you to do anything,' he bit out forcefully. 'I intend dealing with the matter myself!'

Lindsay tidied her desk without really knowing she was doing it, not knowing when Joel said he would 'deal' with it if he meant he would tell Malcolm that the idea of using Marilyn Mills was unthinkable to him, or if he meant he would contact the other woman himself. Jealousy ripped through her at the thought of it being the latter.

'How have you been this week?' Judi looked at her closely, concern in her eyes.

'Busy,' she evaded. The two of them had just returned to her flat from her meeting Judi at the station, the most recent argument with Joel before she had left for the weekend still fresh in her mind.

'And Joel?'

'He's also busy,' she continued to avoid the real subject. 'But I leave in three weeks.'

Judi frowned at this news. 'I thought you said you were going to stay on?'

Lindsay shrugged with a nonchalance she was far from feeling. 'It was a mutual conclusion that I leave after all.'

'How mutual?' her sister asked dryly, guessing the real circumstances.

Lindsay sighed. 'It was an impossible situation. I still love him, but I can't have him on anything but his terms.'

'He would still take you back?'

'I'm not sure he would now,' she answered slowly. 'Things have changed drastically between us this last week.' She went on to explain about Malcolm Reader, and also Marilyn Mills. 'He blames me for the whole thing,' she added dully. 'Thinks I deliberately set out to hurt him.'

'And is he hurt?' Judi prompted softly.

'Well, he certainly isn't the same man who came to my flat a week ago demanding that I went back to him. Then he was defeated but still arrogant. Now he's just angry at everyone and everything.'

'He sounds a complex man—I'd like to meet him,' Judi told her thoughtfully.

'Oh, you will be,' Lindsay assured her innocently.

Her sister's hazel eyes widened in surprise. 'You mean he's coming *here* this weekend?'

'Hardly,' she shook her head, smiling slightly. 'You're going to a dinner party tomorrow night, you'll meet him then. Don't worry,' her smile widened at her sister's concern, 'I shall be there too.'

Judi was frowning now. 'You didn't mention any of this when we spoke on the telephone.'

'Because if I had you would have had time to make up an excuse not to come,' said Lindsay knowingly.

Judi blushed at her correct assessment of the situation. 'You know I don't like these London parties——'

'To my knowledge you've never been to any!'

'No. Well,' she looked disconcerted, 'I still think it was a dirty trick not to have told me sooner.'

'I need you here this weekend, Judi,' Lindsay told her softly. 'Maybe it's selfish of me, but I need you.'

Judi instantly looked contrite. 'Of course I'll come to the dinner party with you—I was just being silly. I'm sure I'll enjoy myself once I get there,' she added doubtfully.

Lindsay laughed ruefully. 'I wish you didn't sound quite so much as if you were being put on the rack!'

'Did I?' Her sister looked chagrined. 'Well, I didn't mean to.' She tried to shake off some of her despondency. 'But I hope you have something I can wear, because I certainly didn't come prepared for a party.'

'Relax, Judi, the one thing your "notorious" sister has plenty of is clothes. I always had to dress the part when I was seen out in public with Joel,' Lindsay added dully.

'And you'll dress the part tomorrow too,' her sister said firmly. 'We'll show Joel Sutherland that you might be down for the moment but you're far from defeated either!'

Lindsay hugged her gratefully. 'I knew I could rely on you to cheer me up!'

But as they prepared for the dinner party the next evening she could tell how nervous Judi really was. Her sister had socialised very little since Jonathan's death, and so this London dinner party must be doubly difficult for her. Lindsay helped her all she could, the two of them going to a hair salon that

afternoon, Judi having her hair restyled silkily to her
shoulders in soft waves, the silky turquoise gown she
and Lindsay had decided she should wear suiting her
fragile beauty perfectly, bringing out the depth of her
hazel eyes.

Lindsay had decided on a sophisticated black dress
for herself, the demure style of the fitted bodice a
startling contrast to the back that dipped to the base of
her spine, the black material flowing freely to her
ankles. It was a dramatic gown, one that allowed for
little to be worn beneath it, a fact that was perfectly
obvious as she moved.

'Well, if that doesn't make Joel Sutherland sit up
and take notice, nothing will!' Judi looked at her with
raised brows, obviously taken aback at what little there
appeared to be of the dress when viewed from the
back.

'I don't want him to take notice.' Lindsay crossly
secured the short straight swathe of her hair behind
one ear with a silver-studded black comb. 'I want him
to leave me alone.'

'In that dress?' Judi looked sceptical.

She turned from her reflection in the mirror. 'For
your information, this is one of Joel's least favourite
dresses.' Her voice was brittle with the memory. 'The
one and only other time I wore it he ordered me to
take it off.' She blushed at Judi's teasing look. 'And
put something else on instead.'

'Oh.'

'Well, don't look so disappointed,' Lindsay said
impatiently. 'Contrary to what everyone says about
affairs, Joel and I did not spend all of our time
together hopping into bed.' Only most of it! She
remembered achingly.

'You didn't have an affair,' Judi told her softly.

'You simply lived with the man you loved. And that's no crime.'

'To some people it is.' Lindsay picked up her bag ready to go.

'Are you all right, Lindsay?' Judi was concerned at the reckless glitter in her eyes. 'We don't have to go——'

'Oh yes, we do,' her sister set her shoulders determinedly. 'Our hostess told me that if I didn't put in an appearance it would look as if I was afraid to. And she's right. So let's go.'

They were far from the first to arrive at Cally and David's London apartment; nevertheless Joel wasn't one of the guests already there, something for which Lindsay was grateful. She would be able to handle the situation so much better if she were firmly established among the crowd when Joel arrived with his girl-friend.

'I'm so glad you could both come,' Cally greeted them enthusiastically. 'And surely your sister *has* to be the model in the family!' She looked appreciatively at the blushing Judi.

'Now don't try and dazzle Judi,' Lindsay laughed. 'She's a self-respecting secretary to a local lawyer back home. And no more interested in modelling than I am.'

Cally looked disappointedly at Judi. 'No?'

'No,' Judi confirmed shyly.

'That's a pity.' Cally drew them both further into the room. 'Still, I'm sure none of my male guests will complain at the two beautiful girls in their midst, no matter what their professions. Now come and meet your dining companions for the evening.'

Lindsay instantly hung back. 'Cally——'

'You said I would cope,' the other woman was

unrepentant. 'And I did—I invited two men to even up the numbers.'

Lindsay frowned. 'I wish you hadn't.'

'You haven't met them yet,' Cally chided lightly.

And she didn't want to either. It hadn't occurred to her that Cally would put them in such an awkward position. And it should have done. It should have done!

Her worst fears were realised as Cally guided them across the room and she saw Malcolm's triumphant grin. But he didn't look any more self-satisfied than Cally did. Damn the other girl and her matchmaking!

Standing next to Malcolm was another American Cally introduced as Glen Shumann, Malcolm's assistant, a tall loose-limbed man with sandy-blond hair, dark blue eyes, and a boyishly handsome face.

'I'll leave you all to get acquainted,' Cally told them brightly after she had made the introductions. 'Enjoy yourselves,' was her parting shot.

'Do you think we will?' Malcolm taunted Lindsay softly as she watched their hostess with angry eyes as she moved like a glittering butterfly among her guests in the yellow and silver dress.

Lindsay gave him an impatient glare. 'You knew all the time that you would be seeing me here tonight——'

'Not true,' he defended lightly. 'Cally didn't call me until yesterday. You're the one who should be reprimanded.'

Her eyes widened indignantly. 'What did I do?'

'You didn't tell me you *had* a sister, let alone that she's so beautiful.'

She had noticed from the start the way Malcolm hadn't been able to take his eyes off Judi, and her sister didn't seem altogether immune to his charms either, blushing like a teenager as she tried to meet his admiring gaze challengingly. Lindsay couldn't remember the last time she had seen Judi look this coy.

But her attention was diverted from this strange phenomenon by a slight stirring of attention towards the door. And she soon saw the reason why. Joel had just arrived, and clinging to his arm like a limpet was Joanne Honeyville, the most popular and successful model of this year.

Joel stood dark and remote as Cally and Joanne chatted together, his evening suit fitting the wide perfection of his shoulders and chest, down to his narrow waist and tapered thighs. He and the tall model made a striking couple, Joanne's dark, almost Oriental colouring perfectly suited to the gold clinging gown she wore. No wonder all eyes were turned towards them!

But if he was aware of the sensation he and Joanne had caused at their entrance he gave no indication of it, his expression one of boredom as his gaze roamed lazily about the room. But all that changed as his gaze passed and then sharply returned to Lindsay, his eyes narrowing as he took in the dress she wore. The last time she had worn it had been the one and only time Joel had shown a hint of possessiveness where she was concerned, declaring it indecent, the perfection of her body clearly shown against its soft material.

But he didn't look possessive tonight, his contemptuous gaze passing from her to Malcolm and then back again, his eyes calling her a liar when she had told him she didn't have a relationship with Malcolm.

CHAPTER FOUR

DAMN him, what right did he have to judge or condemn her even if she *were* seeing Malcolm! It was none of his business what she did any more, in fact it never had been, Joel always making a point of letting her know he had no claims on her. And he had no claims now either, emotional or otherwise, not when he could arrive with Joanne Honeyville clinging to him as if they were already lovers. Maybe they were; Joel had certainly been spending his time with a woman—or women—this last week.

'They make a startling couple, don't they?' Malcolm spoke softly close to her ear.

Lindsay turned sharply, thankfully noting that Judi and Glen weren't also watching her reaction to Joel's arrival, the other couple making light conversation together. 'Very,' she agreed brittlely, her smile bright and meaningless. 'You can always rely on Joel to be with the most beautiful woman in the room.'

'I think that last statement is highly debatable,' he said wolfishly. 'But she's certainly very attractive. I also think I've been acting like a prize fool this last week,' he grimaced.

She frowned, her expression suddenly wary. 'Sorry?'

His smile was gentle. 'I've been walking around with my eyes closed, haven't I?'

Lindsay shook her head. 'I'm sorry, but I still don't understand——'

'It's Joel, isn't it,' he stated softly.

She felt her face drain of all colour, and was grateful for the supporting arm Malcolm slipped about her waist, his hand comforting against her bare back. 'Would you like to sit down?' she suggested breathlessly. 'It's a little warm in here.'

'Sure,' he agreed instantly, nodding their excuses to Judi and Glen, directing her towards the open balcony doors.

Lindsay turned to him laughingly. 'This isn't quite what I had in mind!'

Malcolm guided her to the lounge chair that stood beneath the brightly coloured sun-umbrella; the evening was just beginning to darken to dusk. 'I know that,' he sat down opposite her, 'but I thought we could take these few minutes' respite to cool off.'

'Don't you mean down?'

'I know what I mean,' he said dryly. 'I feel such an ass!'

'I don't know why.' She avoided his gaze.

He sighed. 'It was right there for me to see all the time, and yet I didn't notice a damned thing.'

She shrugged. 'There's been nothing there for you to see since you arrived.'

'But there was,' he grimaced. 'Joel talked about you so warmly when he was in New York, seemed anxious to return to England all the time he was away——'

'I'm sure that anxiety had nothing to do with me,' Lindsay interrupted sharply.

'Oh, I think it did,' Malcolm nodded. 'I made a joking remark about his need to rush back to the special woman in his life and he almost exploded at me!'

'You see?' she sighed. 'I told you it had nothing to do with me.'

'If it didn't he would have laughed it off,' Malcolm

reasoned. 'What happened to break the two of you up?'

She looked at him resentfully. 'You seem pretty sure there was something to break up?'

'And wasn't there?' he prompted softly.

'Only in my mind,' she said bitterly.

'Joel doesn't act like a man who's immune to you,' he derided Joel's behaviour of the last week.

Lindsay blushed slightly. 'I didn't say he doesn't desire me, I know that he does—or did,' she amended softly.

'Does,' Malcolm said firmly.

She shrugged. 'Maybe he still does,' she sighed agreement. 'But it makes no difference.'

'To what?'

'To the fact that we aren't compatible!'

Malcolm smiled slightly. 'How many people are, when it really comes down to it?' he dismissed. 'I'm afraid love has no discrimination, it just is, and there isn't a thing any of us can do about it.'

She knew that, had known from the first that Joel was a hard and insensitive man, that he could be cruel when it came to protecting his own feelings. And yet knowing that hadn't stopped her loving him. 'There was no love involved in our relationship,' she told Malcolm abruptly. 'We just lived together for six months, and now it's over.'

'Ah,' he said thoughtfully.

'What do you mean, "ah"?' she demanded impatiently.

'You and Joel lived together?' he answered her question with one of his own.

'Shocking, isn't it?' she said with self-derisive bitterness. 'A well brought up young lady like me "living in sin" with a man!'

'And was it? Sinful, I mean?' Malcolm teased.

'Incredibly,' she revealed longingly, remembering the long languorous nights of passion she had spent in Joel's arms.

'He was your first lover?'

Lindsay stiffened at how personal he had become. 'Really, Malcolm, I don't think——'

'No, don't think,' he encouraged softly. 'Just answer me.' He looked at her with probing eyes.

She swallowed hard, moistening her lips. 'Yes, he was,' she told him agitatedly. 'But if you think that meant anything to him, don't. He got a tremendous kick out of knowing he was the first, but it really wasn't that important to him, in fact I'm sure he would rather I'd been more experienced. You and he are very much alike in some ways, neither of you wants a permanent commitment.'

'You're wrong.'

'No, I——'

'About me, I mean,' he cut in gently. 'I can't speak for Joel, I don't know what his hang-up is——'

'He doesn't have one,' she assured him bitterly.

'Oh yes,' the other man nodded, 'he has one. But whatever it is I don't have it. I've been looking for forty-one years to find the other half of myself. And I can't settle for second best, no matter how beautiful or nice the woman is. I want the woman who was meant just for me.'

'You're a romantic!'

'So are you, under all that cynicism that's rubbed off on you from Joel.' His hand covered both of hers as they rested in her lap. 'If he's the one you want you should fight for him, not leave him in the clutches of other women.'

Her mouth twisted. 'I think you have that the

wrong way around,' she derided. 'Joel controls all his relationships.'

'Is that why he's been glaring at me as if he would like to see me dead?'

She flushed. 'That's my fault, I'm afraid, I told him you and I weren't going out together. I had no idea Cally was going to invite you here tonight,' she added dully.

'If Joel doesn't care about you why should he be interested?' Malcolm raised dark brows.

'You don't understand——'

'I think it's you who doesn't understand, Lindsay. Take it from one of his own sex, Joel is a very confused man at the moment.'

'He looks it,' she mocked.

'Believe me, Lindsay——'

'Ah, there you both are,' Cally spied them on the balcony. 'I thought two of my guests had absconded already!'

Malcolm had stood up as soon as the other woman joined them on the balcony, retaining a hold of one of Lindsay's hands to pull her up beside him. 'I just wanted to be alone with this lovely lady for a few minutes,' he explained smoothly.

Cally looked pleased that her matchmaking was going so well. 'We'll be going in to dinner in a few minutes, so if you wouldn't mind . . .' she added pointedly.

'Not at all.' He put Lindsay's hand firmly in the crook of his arm, holding it there with his other hand. 'I hope you've seated me next to Lindsay.'

'But of course,' Cally smiled at them both.

Lindsay had no idea what Malcolm was trying to do, but she was grateful for his support as they returned to the lounge under the cold stare of tawny eyes. Joel was surrounded by attentive women and men as usual, one of those people that, however taciturn themselves, still managed to attract people to him, and he looked as if he were being at his remotest this evening, adding nothing to the conversation about him, drinking steadily from the glass of whisky in his hand.

'Does he get legless or just unpleasant?' Malcolm spoke close to her ear as they went through to the dining-room.

Lindsay didn't pretend to misunderstand him. 'He stays exactly as he is.'

'What a pity,' said Malcolm with relish. 'I would have liked to have seen him lose a little of that control.'

As far as she knew there was only one occasion when Joel lost his inhibitions enough to let someone else control *him*, and then he was intoxicated with desire, not alcohol! Under his teaching she had learnt to please him, to occasionally be the aggressor in their lovemaking, but as if seeing it as a weakness Joel usually held back at those times, being much more comfortable when he controlled their passion.

'Excuse me for a moment while I just have a word with Judi,' she said hastily, knowing that Malcolm was astute enough to read her thoughts. 'I feel a little guilty for deserting her as we did.'

'She doesn't look in need of your moral support,' Malcolm remarked dryly.

Lindsay looked across the room to where Judi was in animated conversation with Glen Shumann. 'No, she doesn't does she?' she realised with amusement, relieved that her sister was getting on so well with the other man. In her agitation at seeing Joel she had selfishly forgotten all about Judi's welfare, allowing herself to be taken outside by Malcolm without a second thought for her sister. 'Still, I'll just check that she's all right, if you don't mind.'

'Go right ahead,' he invited.

Judi was flushed and more beautiful than Lindsay had seen her in a long time, her eyes glowing as she turned to look at her sister. 'I'm fine,' she assured Lindsay at her apologetic query. 'Glen has been looking after me.'

Lindsay raised blonde brows. 'I can see that.'

Judi gave her a derisive glance. 'He's been telling me all about his wife and two children in America.'

'Oh,' she looked confused.

Judi laughed softly, obviously enjoying herself. 'And how much he misses them,' she added mischievously.

'Oh,' said Lindsay again, feeling a little foolish. 'I didn't realise,' she spoke to Glen. 'I mean, I had no idea——'

'Your sister is a very sympathetic listener,' he gave an understanding smile.

'Well, as long as you're sure you're all right?' she prompted Judi.

'I'm fine,' her sister nodded. 'But about Joel,' she added in a conspiratorial whisper. 'Which one is he?'

Lindsay blushed as Glen gave her a curious look. 'Judi, could we talk about this later——'

'Good evening, Lindsay,' a harsh voice grated softly. 'Aren't you going to introduce me to your friend?'

She turned slowly, aware that her cheeks had gone first red and then pale, her eyes suddenly luminous. Joel stood alone, strangely still and dangerous, a watchful air about him. 'Aren't you going to introduce us to yours?' The bitchy comment came out before she could stop herself.

His mouth twisted derisively. 'Joanne is being dazzled by the world of politics at the moment,' he looked pointedly across the room to where the model was deep in conversation with David Robin, their host.

'So being at a loose end for a few minutes you thought you would come over and be introduced to the only female you don't know in the room?' Her mockery was brittle. 'How nice!'

His eyes had narrowed to icy slits. 'What the hell is the matter with you——'

'You must be Joel,' Judi interrupted brightly, putting out her hand in a friendly gesture. 'I'm Judi Pope.'

Joel slowly took the offered hand. 'Pope . . .?'

'I'm Lindsay's sister,' she explained lightly.

His gaze flickered briefly over Lindsay before moving back to Judi, a charming smile suddenly relaxing his harsh features. 'Lindsay didn't tell me how beautiful you are, otherwise I might have taken her up on her offer to meet her family,' he said smoothly.

Lindsay felt what little colour there was leave her face, her body went rigid. God, he was a cruel bastard, flirting with her own sister in a way designed to hurt her.

Judi met his gaze unflinchingly. 'We're a very dull lot, I'm afraid,' she told him evenly. 'Lindsay is the adventurous one in our family—and not always with happy results,' she added challengingly.

Joel's mouth tightened at the intended insult. 'Really?'

'Yes—really,' her friendly smile didn't take the sting out of her words. 'I'm so glad to have had this opportunity to meet you, Mr Sutherland,' she said dismissively. 'It's been an—enlightening experience. Now if you'll excuse us, Glen and I are going to take our places at the table.' She walked away with great dignity, a bewildered Glen following in her wake.

Joel watched her with an appreciative gleam in his eyes. 'You didn't tell me about the family resemblance,' he remarked softly to Lindsay.

'Our colouring is very——'

'Not the colouring,' he looked down at her with enigmatically gold eyes. 'Judi's tongue is as sharp as yours.'

She stiffened. 'I'm sure she didn't mean anything by it.'

'And I'm equally sure she did,' he said with amusement. 'I liked her.'

'I'm sure she'll be glad to hear it,' Lindsay snapped tightly.

He sobered as he looked down at her. 'Lindsay, why are we doing this to each other? I still want you, and I'd swear you still want me,' his voice had lowered seductively. 'Why don't we make our excuses right now and go back to my apartment?'

'To your bed, you mean?' she amended waspishly.

'God, yes,' he groaned huskily.

Her eyes flashed with anger. 'You might be able to solve all your problems between the sheets, Joel, but you certainly can't solve mine!'

'I could try,' he encouraged throatily. 'I always could in the past.'

'No, I——'

'Cally's waiting for us to sit down, honey.' Malcolm appeared at her side, his arm possessive about her waist. 'Hi, Joel,' he greeted the other man in a friendly voice, just as if he didn't know he had interrupted a very private conversation. 'I think your girl-friend is looking for you.'

Joel's hand came out to clasp Lindsay's arm. 'What's your answer?' He ignored the other man.

She looked straight up at Malcolm. 'Dinner sounds like a good idea,' she said lightly. 'Perhaps we'll see you later, Joel,' she turned back to him. 'You *and* Miss Honeyville.' Her head was high as she allowed Malcolm to escort her to the table, where Judi was sitting at Malcolm's other side, Glen next to her.

'Propositioning you, was he?' Malcolm said softly.

'You could say that,' she answered vaguely, pretending not to notice as Joel was seated at the opposite end of the table, sitting on Cally's left, Joanne at his side.

'He doesn't want to let go, does he?' Malcolm looked thoughtful.

She flashed him an irritated look. 'He doesn't like being told no, you mean.'

His mouth quirked with amusement. 'I'm sure it must be a novelty.' He looked pointedly down the table to where several women were trying to gain Joel's attention, while he morosely ignored them all.

'Yes,' Lindsay acknowledged waspishly.

He eyed her curiously. 'Is that why you said it?'

'Said what?' she frowned her impatience, wishing he would talk about something else, anything else.

'No. Walking out on him was guaranteed to make him either go all out to get you back or go out with a number of other women to salvage his pride.'

She sipped the wine that had just been poured for her with agitated movements. 'Then it must be obvious which one he chose!'

'Or was forced to choose.' He gave a rueful shrug at her disbelieving snort. 'Joel comes over to me as a man with a lot on his mind—and not all of it pleasant.'

'Even less so since you gave him the problem of Marilyn Mills to think over!' she derided.

'Changing the subject?' he murmured.

She grimaced. 'How did you guess?'

'Oh, just male intuition, I guess,' he said self-derisively. 'Okay, I've probed enough for one night. But who would have guessed there was a powder-keg boiling under such a cool façade?'

'Joel?' she frowned.

'You,' he mused. 'It's almost worth cancelling my return to the States to see how this puzzle works out.'

'You're leaving?'

'Not yet,' he shrugged. 'But soon.'

'Well, don't delay on our account, our puzzle has already ended.'

'You sounded very firm when you said that?'

'I am.' She looked at him with challenge.

Malcolm stared straight back at her for several timeless seconds, then he nodded. 'If you don't want to discuss Joel any more let's go on to another interesting subject.'

Lindsay could feel the tension leaving her body at his acceptance of her wishes, knowing he could be even more determined than her if he chose to be. 'Such as?' she prompted lightly.

'Judi.' He glanced fleetingly at her sister as she still talked avidly to Glen, obviously enjoying herself despite her earlier misgivings. 'Tell me about Judi,' he invited huskily.

She smiled, knowing now that she had been right about his interest in her sister earlier. 'She's my older sister by two years, is kind to animals and elderly people, works as a secretary, and lives at home with my mother and younger brother.'

Malcolm shook his head. 'I could have got all that from Judi herself. I want to know what happened to put the shadows in her eyes.'

Lindsay sobered at his perception. 'That's something Judi *will* have to tell you—if she wants to.'

He grimaced. 'Do you think I would come under the heading of "kind to elderly people"?'

She laughed softly. 'I doubt it.'

'I didn't think so,' he said ruefully.

'Although that doesn't mean you shouldn't try to gain her confidence,' she added quickly.

His eyes widened with renewed interest. 'You think I could?'

Lindsay smiled gently, knowing he really was genuinely attracted to Judi. And he was sensitive enough to have realised she had been hurt in the past, he wasn't the type of man who would deliberately see her hurt again. 'I think it's worth a try. Now eat your dinner,' she encouraged lightly, aware that they were the last to finish the first course. 'We're holding everyone up,' she blushed as she looked up and found hard tawny eyes on her.

She was still a little shaken from that encounter with Joel before dinner; she had been unprepared for him to ask her back to his apartment in that way. And if she had been prepared? Her answer would still have had to be the same, no matter how tempted she was to say yes, to take one more night in his arms.

'That doesn't mean we have to stop talking altogether,' Malcolm mocked her continued silence during the meal.

She blushed lightly. 'Sorry. I was—I was deep in thought.'

His mouth twisted. 'I can guess about what.'

She gave a guilty shrug. 'I haven't thanked you yet for coming to my assistance earlier.'

'Think nothing of it,' he dismissed. 'To make up for it you can help me get to know your sister better later.'

'I'd be glad to,' Lindsay smiled.

Dinner was a long-drawn-out affair, the guests a curious mixture of Cally's friends from her modelling days and David's political friends, the two somehow seeming to make scintillating company. And if Joel hadn't been there Lindsay was sure she would have enjoyed herself immensely. But he was there, and she was aware of his every move, stiffened with distress and jealousy every time Joanne touched him with scarlet-tipped fingers.

'It can eat you up alive, you know,' Malcolm murmured as they went back to the lounge after the meal.

She shot him a sharp look. 'I can't help the way I feel.'

'Maybe not, but you could try giving him back the same treatment.'

'Are you offering your services?' she mused.

'Why not?' he shrugged. 'He's already as mad as hell at both of us.'

'And Judi wouldn't understand at all,' she told him pointedly, aware of the surreptitious looks her sister had been shooting Malcolm during the meal, blushing like a schoolgirl if he should happen to speak to her.

Malcolm's eyes were a warm blue. 'Your sister is a sweet and unusual lady.'

'Yes, she is,' she agreed unhesitant. 'And I want to see her happy, thinking there's something between the two of us could only complicate matters, don't you think?' She eyed him mockingly.

He looked disconcerted by her candour, and then he gave a rueful grin. 'You're a very astute young lady,' he murmured finally.

'Just very fond of my sister,' she corrected softly.

'You think I stand a chance with her?'

'I think you have a better one if I don't complicate things for you,' she told him cautiously, knowing how reluctant Judi was to become emotionally involved with anyone since Jonathan, no matter how coy her reaction was to Malcolm.

'Cally mentioned that Judi is staying the weekend with you . . .?'

'Yes?' she gave him a teasing smile. 'What did you have in mind?'

'Would the two of you like to spend the day with me tomorrow?'

Lindsay laughed softly. 'Why don't you just ask Judi out on your own?'

'She may not come,' he answered honestly.

It was strangely endearing to see this normally self-confident man so vulnerable. 'All right,' she agreed softly. 'We could drive out and have lunch somewhere.'

He leant forward and kissed her gently on the mouth. 'Thank you.'

There was no doubting his sincerity where Judi was concerned, his genuine desire to get to know her. But as Lindsay looked across the room and met Joel's coldly contemptuous gaze she wished he hadn't been quite so exuberant in his gratitude!

'So how did you like your first London dinner party?' Lindsay teased her sister as they lay in bed later that night.

'It was—interesting,' Judi answered cautiously.

Her brows rose. 'I thought you enjoyed yourself. You seemed to be getting on well with Glen.'

'Yes.'

Lindsay looked across the darkened room to where Judi lay in the adjoining single bed, wondering at the reserve in her sister's voice. 'But?'

Judi shrugged. 'Well, he is married, and I wouldn't like anyone to have got the wrong idea——'

'Of course they didn't,' she denied laughingly. 'And what did you think of Malcolm?' she asked casually.

'He seemed very nice.'

'That's good, because we're going out with him for the day tomorrow.'

'Both of us?'

'Yes,' Lindsay nodded.

'What about Glen?'

'Malcolm didn't mention him,' she shook her head.

'Then I'd rather not go either,' Judi said firmly.

'Why on earth not?'

'I don't want to intrude.'

'You won't be. Judi, what did you really think of Malcolm?' Lindsay probed gently.

'I thought he was—very attractive,' Judi admitted after several seconds.

Lindsay turned over tiredly. 'Good,' she murmured in a pleased voice.

'What do you mean, good?' Judi demanded sharply. 'Lindsay? Lindsay . . .!'

She continued to pretend to be asleep, having effectively found out that Judi was attracted to Malcolm too, while avoiding the subject of Joel. She didn't want to talk about him any more tonight, felt drained from talking about him with Malcolm. The fact that he had left early with the clinging Joanne didn't help the turmoil of her emotions; she was able to imagine the two of them together now, Joel's dark head resting against Joanne's ivory skin.

Malcolm arrived early to take them out the next morning, and Lindsay made her excuses as soon as he did. 'I have a headache,' she told them both regretfully.

'Then I'll stay here with you,' offered Judi instantly.

'There's no point,' she said gently. 'Why don't the two of you go for a nice drive?'

Her sister blushed uncomfortably, very slender and attractive in fitted brown trousers and a vest tee-shirt. 'I wouldn't hear of it—I'll stay and take care of you.'

'I'll only be lying down,' Lindsay insisted, 'so there won't be anything to take care of.'

'But——'

'Go and get your jacket,' she ordered. 'We can't keep Malcolm waiting all day when he's been kind enough to offer to take us out.'

Judi shot her a resentful glare before striding angrily into the bedroom and slamming the door behind her.

'Do you really have a headache?' Malcolm asked ruefully.

'As it happens, yes.' Lindsay pulled a face, not having slept well at all the night before.

'I don't think Judi believes you.'

'Would you?' she derided.

'No,' he still grimaced. 'She has quite a temper, doesn't she?' he said admiringly.

'We both do. Still want to be alone with her?' Lindsay mocked softly.

'I'll find a way to calm her down,' he said with anticipation.

From the thunderous expression on Judi's face

when she returned from the bedroom it wasn't going to be easy! Lindsay watched them leave with amusement, her humour fading as soon as she was alone, her headache the result of not being able to rid herself of the mental image of Joel and Joanne together, her torment agony as she knew it could have been her in his arms.

It was the slamming of the apartment door that woke her from the disturbed sleep she had drifted into as she lay on the sofa, sitting up with a start as Judi stormed through to the bedroom. There was no evidence of Malcolm following her, so Lindsay could only assume the two of them had argued. Not a good start to their relationship.

A glance at her wrist-watch told her that the other couple had only been gone a couple of hours. What on earth had Malcolm done to upset her sister in that short time?

Judi was packing her weekend case when Lindsay went into the bedroom. 'What's going on?' She sat down on the opposite bed to watch her sister's agitated movements.

'What does it look like?' Judi snapped.

'But you don't leave for hours yet,' she frowned, still a little groggy from her nap.

'I've decided to take the earlier train,' Judi told her tightly. Lindsay's frown deepened. 'Why?'

Judi stopped the frantic packing of her case long enough to sit down heavily on the bed. 'I know you like living here, that you enjoy the pace and excitement of it all. But I don't understand it or the people!'

'Judi, you aren't making sense,' she prompted softly.

Tears filled the disturbed hazel eyes. 'It wasn't even

my fault. I did nothing to encourage him. But he just——'

'Are we talking about Malcolm?' Lindsay asked in bewilderment.

'Of course we're talking about Malcolm,' Judi confirmed impatiently. 'I don't know why you encouraged me to go out with him alone in the first place. I realise that after Mother disapproved so strongly of Joel you probably wanted someone on your side this time, but——'

'Judi, what are you talking about?' She was sure it couldn't just be the last remnants of sleep that were making this conversation impossible to follow; Judi really wasn't making any sense!

'You and Malcolm!'

'Malcolm and—I?' Lindsay repeated slowly.

'And I really did like him to begin with,' her sister continued agitatedly. 'But I think you should know that he—well, he isn't quite as charming as he seems,' she concluded awkwardly.

The amusement of the situation began to dawn on Lindsay. 'No?'

'No,' she seemed reluctant to elucidate on that point.

'What did he do, make a pass at you?' Lindsay asked with relish, sure from Judi's reaction that that was *exactly* what he had done. His method of 'calming' her sister down seemed to have had the opposite effect!

'It isn't funny, Lindsay,' Judi groaned her dismay. 'Although I'm glad you can see something amusing in the fact that your boy-friend made a pass at your own sister!' she added disgustedly.

'Oh, but I wouldn't find that funny at all,' Lindsay disagreed.

Judi gave her an impatient glare. 'Then I suppose I'm imagining that silly smile on your face?'

Her humour deepened. 'Not at all.'

'Lindsay——'

'Darling, Malcolm isn't my boy-friend,' Lindsay gently interrupted the angry tirade that had been about to begin. 'He's someone who's turning out to be a very good friend, but I very much think it's you he's romantically interested in.'

'Me . . .?' her sister echoed dazedly.

'Judi, surely it was obvious! Why do you think I tried to find out what you thought of him last night?' she derided.

'I thought you wanted my approval——'

'I do,' Lindsay confirmed forcefully, amazed that her sister had gained the wrong impression anyway. 'I like Malcolm very much, and I think you'll be good for each other.'

'No,' Judi shook her head dully.

'We all cared about Jonathan, love, but you're only twenty-four, you can't spend the rest of your life tied to a memory,' Lindsay pointed out gently.

'It isn't that,' her sister choked. 'Jonathan would have been the first one to encourage me to find happiness. But I made such an idiot of myself with Malcolm today that I'll never be able to face him again!' she groaned.

'Never is a long time. Tell me exactly what happened,' Lindsay encouraged.

'Well, he was very warm and friendly—too much so, I thought, so I was frosty with him——'

'Very loyal of you,' Lindsay teased.

'If you aren't going to take this seriously——'

'Oh, I am, I am,' she soothed her sister. 'What happened to make you storm in here half an hour ago?'

Judi seemed embarrassed just thinking about it. 'He—he kissed me,' she revealed reluctantly.

'I would have thought that was very natural in the circumstances,' nodded Lindsay, waiting for the rest.

'And that's when I hit him,' Judi continued gloomily.

'Oh.' Lindsay held back her smile with difficulty, wondering what Malcolm's reaction had been to that. It seemed he hadn't had time to make one!

'Then I called him every foul name I knew—and a few more I didn't even understand!—and demanded that he bring me home immediately. If you don't stop laughing, Lindsay,' she warned through gritted teeth, 'I'm likely to hit you too!'

'My, you are violent today!' Lindsay sobered from her uncontrollable laughter as Judi continued to look fierce. 'The poor man kissed you because he's attracted to you.'

'Well, I didn't know that!'

'I would have thought it was obvious.'

'What was obvious was that the two of you spent the whole of yesterday evening together,' Judi snapped. 'Even sneaking out on to the balcony so that you could be alone together. I even saw him kiss you once!'

'He was thanking me for approving and encouraging his interest in you,' Lindsay derided.

'Well, I couldn't be expected to know that!'

'You do now, so what are you going to do about it?' she asked curiously.

'Nothing,' her sister said stubbornly.

'Judi——'

'I mean it,' she cut in firmly. 'I'd be too embarrassed to explain the mistake I made.'

'Malcolm won't mind,' Lindsay assured her sister confidently.

'Well, I do. I made an idiot of myself, and I don't intend adding to it by seeing him again.'

'So you're going to go back home and act as if you had never met him,' said Lindsay with impatience. 'You're just being stubborn, Judi.'

'I'm being stubborn?' her sister scorned. 'And what would you call what you've been about Joel?'

She stiffened warily. 'Joel?'

'Yes—Joel,' Judi repeated determinedly.

'What about him?' she asked defensively.

'It's blatantly obvious that the two of you are still extremely attracted to each other——'

'Attraction doesn't make love,' Lindsay dismissed abruptly.

'It makes the beginning of love——'

'After six months I think we know it isn't love on his side,' Lindsay scorned harshly.

'That's another thing—the way you talked about him I had the impression of a selfish monster only interested in getting you into bed with him and nothing else——'

'That is all he's interested in!'

'Rubbish!' Judi told her impatiently. 'He stared at the balcony doors for fifteen solid minutes while you were outside with Malcolm—that doesn't give me the impression of a man only interested in sex.'

'You sound as if you're defending him!' accused Lindsay.

'I feel sorry for him.'

'He doesn't need your pity,' she derided. 'Especially when he has women like Joanne Honeyville around.'

'She didn't mean anything to him, he didn't even notice she was there half the time.'

'Well, I did! I thought you were on my side, Judi,'

said Lindsay in a hurt voice. 'You didn't seem to like him last night,' she remembered.

'I admit I had a little natural defence of my sister, but that doesn't mean I didn't like him. There's something about him, something that troubles him deeply.'

Lindsay stood up, moving with agitated movements. 'Why is it that everyone suspects Joel of having a motive for the way he is?' she demanded to know angrily. 'Why can't any of you accept the fact that he's a selfish bastard and leave it at that?'

'Because he isn't, not basically,' Judi told her gently. 'And you don't believe he is either.'

No, but then she knew Joel's aversion to love was somehow connected with Marilyn Mills, and she hated the other woman for it. 'Don't presume to lecture me, Judi, when you're too stubborn to make your own peace with Malcolm,' she said waspishly. 'I don't want us to fall out about this, but it's just too painful to keep talking about,' she added raggedly.

'I'm sorry, love,' Judi was instantly contrite. 'I know I shouldn't try and interfere. I just don't like to see you unhappy.'

'I'll get over it.' Lindsay said flatly.

But it was an empty promise, she knew that. Maybe if, like Jonathan, Joel had been taken from her by death, she might have eventually been able to fall in love again. But not when he was so close to her physically and so far away emotionally, then it was impossible to forget him or the love she had for him.

But there was one thing she knew about Judi that her sister didn't; she was going to find love again whether she wanted it or not! Lindsay thought she knew Malcolm well enough by now to know he wouldn't be put off by a slap on the cheek and a few abusive words. He was going to be a very welcome member of the family.

CHAPTER FIVE

'ARE you getting all the excitement you want out of life now?' Joel rasped as he came into Lindsay's office first thing Monday morning.

'Sorry?' she asked guardedly.

He came to sit on the edge of her desk, his grey fitted trousers taut against his muscled thighs, his black shirt giving him a satanic look. 'As I remember it, one of the things you said was missing from our relationship was fun and excitement,' he drawled contemptuously.

She flushed. 'I didn't say that exactly——'

'Your exact words were that I never took you anywhere that was fun or exciting,' he recalled harshly. 'Does Malcolm take you to exciting places?'

'Joel——'

'Or do you find it exciting enough just to be with him?' he cut in coldly. 'I noticed he's already had the one privilege you never allowed me.'

Lindsay was very pale at this unwarranted attack. 'What's that?' she asked numbly.

'Staying overnight at your apartment!'

She frowned. 'Don't be ridiculous!'

'I saw his car outside your home yesterday morning, Lindsay,' he insisted accusingly. 'So don't attempt to deny it.'

Her apartment was at the opposite end of town to Joel's, so he couldn't have driven by it by accident. Unless, of course, Joanne Honeyville's home was at the same end of town as hers! 'Don't judge everyone by your own standards, Joel,' she snapped. 'Malcolm's car may have been parked outside my home, but he certainly hadn't stayed the night. You taught me well and pleasurably, Joel, but I'm certainly not into the *ménage à trois* league.'

His eyes narrowed to icy slits. 'What do you mean?'

'My sister stayed with me last night,' she told him bitterly. 'I think it would have been a little crowded if Malcolm had stayed too!'

Joel looked disconcerted now, her answer obviously surprising him. 'You can't imagine what thoughts went through my mind when I saw his car there,' he said raggedly.

'Oh, but I can,' she sighed. 'Knowing you.'

'Lindsay——'

She pulled her hand out of his grasp. 'Don't touch me!' she glared at him with glittering eyes.

He looked taken aback by her vehemence. 'I was only going to say I was sorry,' he said slowly.

Lindsay flushed awkwardly. 'Apology accepted,' she bit out. 'Now Colette is waiting in your studio for you,' she said briskly. 'She's been waiting some time,' she added pointedly.

A shutter came down over his arrogant features as he stood up. 'Maybe now she knows how I feel when she turns up late for a session,' he dismissed his own lateness this morning.

Lindsay felt the tension leave her once she was alone again, disconcerted by the fact that Joel had seen Malcolm's car outside her home and misconstrued the reason for it. Although his own reason for being in that part of town at that time of morning was suspect, certainly it gave him no right to judge her morals, even erroneously.

But the fact that he was completely wrong about

Malcolm and herself was none of his business, although if he could have heard Malcolm's worried telephone call to her the previous evening he would be in no doubt where the other man's interest lay. Malcolm had been frantic with worry that he had alienated Judi irrevocably, not finding it in the least funny when she explained the humour of the situation to him. In the end she just gave him Judi's telephone number and left them to it. She wasn't capable of sorting out her own love life, let alone anyone else's!

With only three weeks left now until she was unemployed she got down to the serious business of finding herself another job, soon finding that wasn't very easy. Nevertheless, she did manage to get a couple of interviews for later in the week, knowing that far from assured her of getting one of the jobs. But she couldn't go home, she just couldn't.

Her telephone was ringing madly when she got in just after seven that evening, Joel keeping her working late, something she had become used to the last year, although for the last six months those late nights had meant a leisurely dinner together out somewhere. She was going to miss those dinners.

'Yes?' Her voice was rather breathless after she had rushed to answer the telephone.

'Traitor!' came the instant angry hiss.

It was the first touch of humour she had known all day, and she smiled to herself. 'Judi, how nice of you to call and thank me for the weekend,' she taunted her sister. 'I enjoyed it too.'

'And you're enjoying yourself right now too,' her sister accused heatedly.

'What do you mean?' Lindsay pretended an innocence they both knew she was far from feeling.

'Malcolm Reader is in the lounge at this very moment, charming Mother silly!'

He certainly hadn't lost any time! 'In that case I take it you're using the extension in the kitchen?' said Lindsay with interest.

'You know very well I am,' Judi replied agitatedly. 'It isn't enough that he's been ringing me all day—oh no, he has to be waiting in the house when I get home. He had the gall to tell Mother he's a friend of mine!'

'And isn't he?'

'No!'

Poor Judi, she wasn't used to anyone ordering her life in this way, and Lindsay couldn't resist teasing her some more. 'If I were you I'd get back in there before they decide what colour the bridesmaids are going to wear and what hymns will be sung at the church!'

'Well, if you're expecting to be one of my bridesmaids you can forget it!' Judi slammed down the receiver.

Lindsay smiled to herself. Judi didn't know what an admission she had just made with that last statement, or she would never have made it. And she could just see Malcolm charming their mother; he would be exactly the type of son-in-law she would welcome into the family, rich and easygoing, everything that Joel had never been and never would be.

Joel. Every thought she had, happy or sad, led back to him. And it couldn't go on. Although, the way Joel reacted the next day to her request for time off later that afternoon to go for an interview, one would imagine she wasn't allowed to think of anything else *but* him!

'You're working your notice, Lindsay,' he snapped, poring over some photographs he had just developed as they lay strewn across his desk. 'Not using this studio as a holiday camp!'

'Most employers——'

'I'm not most employers,' he bit out coldly. 'I would have thought you would have learnt that by now. How am I supposed to manage here while you're out getting yourself a new job?'

'Don't tell me you're actually admitting to needing someone?' Lindsay was stung into replying, having needed all her courage to ask for this time off in the first place.

His eyes were icy chips as his gaze slowly moved over her. 'You're right, of course. I managed before you came, and I'll manage after you've gone too.'

His double meaning wasn't lost on her. But he needn't have worried; she had no illusions about her importance in his life. 'Can I have the time off or not?' she asked tightly. 'If it makes you feel any happier,' she added with sarcasm, 'I can take my lunch-hour then.'

Joel's mouth twisted derisively. 'Trying to make me feel guilty, Lindsay?'

She shook her head. 'I'm well aware that would do no good!'

His mouth tightened. 'You haven't always thought me such a selfish bastard.'

'Haven't I?' She met his gaze challengingly.

'Then why the hell did you move in with me?' he rasped with barely leashed savagery.

'Curiosity!'

'Curiosity?' he repeated softly, dangerously.

'Maybe I wanted to find out for myself if everything they said about Joel Sutherland, the lover, was true!'

'Bitchiness doesn't become you, Lindsay,' he told her coldly. 'And neither does lying.'

YOURS FREE FOR KEEPS!

Use the edge of a coin to rub off the box at right and reveal your surprise gift ➡

DEAR READER:

We would like to send you 4 Harlequin Presents just like the one you're reading plus a surprise gift – all **ABSOLUTELY FREE.**

If you like them, we'll send you 6 more books each month to preview. Always before they're available in stores. Always for less than the regular retail price. Always with the right to cancel and owe nothing.

In addition, you'll receive **FREE**...
• our monthly newsletter HEART TO HEART
• our magazine ROMANCE DIGEST
• fabulous bonus books and surprise gifts
• special-edition Harlequin Bestsellers to preview for ten days without obligation

So return the attached Card and start your Harlequin honeymoon today.

Sincerely

Pamela Powers
Pamela Powers
for Harlequin

P.S. Remember, your 4 free novels and your surprise gift are yours to keep whether you buy any books or not.

PRINTED IN U.S.A.

4 EXCITING ROMANCE NOVELS PLUS A SURPRISE GIFT

FREE BOOKS/ SURPRISE GIFT

YES, please send me my four **FREE** Harlequin Presents® and my **FREE** surprise gift. Then send me six brand-new Harlequin Presents each month as soon as they come off the presses. Bill me at the low price of $1.75 each (for a total of $10.50 — a saving of $1.20 off the retail price). There are no shipping, handling or other hidden costs. There is no minimum number of books I must purchase. I can always return a shipment and cancel at any time. Even if I never buy a book from Harlequin, the four free novels and the surprise gift are mine to keep forever.

106 CIP BA5T

NAME_____

ADDRESS_____APT. NO._____

CITY_____

STATE_____ZIP_____

Offer limited to one per household and not valid for present subscribers. Prices subject to change.

Mail to:

Harlequin Reader Service
2504 W. Southern Avenue,
Tempe, Arizona 85282

LIMITED TIME ONLY
Mail today and get a
SECOND MYSTERY GIFT

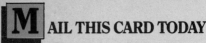

M AIL THIS CARD TODAY

You'll receive 4 Harlequin novels
plus a fabulous surprise gift
ABSOLUTELY FREE

BUSINESS REPLY CARD

First Class   Permit No. 70   Tempe, AZ

Postage will be paid by addressee

Harlequin Reader Service
2504 W. Southern Avenue
Tempe, Arizona 85282

She stiffened. 'Why should I lie?'

He swung away from her. 'How the hell do I know? What do I really know about you?' he muttered.

She was surprised at this, and showed it. 'But I'm an open book,' she frowned.

'I started to read that book once,' he scorned harshly. 'I never did get to the end of *War and Peace*!'

'I hadn't realised I was that boring,' Lindsay snapped shrilly.

'You aren't boring,' Joel taunted. 'I'm only just beginning to realise how complex you are. Hell, take the time off for your interview,' he dismissed with impatience. 'I'm sure you will, anyway.'

She shook her head. 'Not if you don't want me to,' she assured him quietly.

'By all means get yourself another job,' he mocked. 'Just what is this interview for?'

'Secretary,' she supplied uninformatively.

'Don't be so unco-operative, Lindsay,' he taunted confidently. 'You'll need a reference from me, won't you?'

She flushed at the logic of that. Of course she was going to need a reference from him. 'It's with an advertising agency,' she supplied reluctantly.

Joel's eyes narrowed to thoughtful slits. 'Which one?' He gave an appreciative nod as she told him the name of one of the top agencies in town. 'I thought you were looking for something a little more—routine,' he drawled.

'It appears that beggars can't be choosers,' she dismissed.

His expression darkened. 'Why don't you just stay on here?'

'Because it wouldn't work—doesn't work,' she told him huskily.

'God, woman, you don't have to walk out on a perfectly good job just because a love affair turns sour,' he scorned.

'Our affair had nothing to do with love, Joel,' she informed him tightly. 'And all I'm doing now is reverting to the original plans I made six months ago, and that was to leave.'

'You're a fool.'

'So I believe,' she nodded.

'A stubborn fool,' he amended pointedly.

She gave a slight smile. '"The pot calling the kettle black", Joel?'

'Probably,' he drawled acknowledgement of the fact. 'I'll talk to Paul Robards about you later this morning.'

She knew Paul Robards was the head of the advertising agency she was going to, what she hadn't known was that Joel was so friendly with him that he could call him and talk to him personally. 'I'd rather you didn't,' she said stiffly.

His eyes narrowed at her suddenly abrupt manner. 'Why not?' he prompted softly.

She shrugged. 'What would you tell him?' she asked bitterly. 'What an efficient secretary I am, and how I'm not averse to—working, after hours?'

'Lindsay——!'

Lindsay gave a weary sigh. 'Well, it's the truth, isn't it?' she said dully.

Joel's face was pale, his expression haggard. 'The relationship we had outside this office,' he told her between clenched teeth, 'was no one's business but our own.'

'Oh, of course, silly me!' Her tone contained sarcasm. 'You didn't want anyone to know about the two of us then, so why should you want to broadcast it now?'

'Lindsay——'

'Thank you for the time off, Joel,' she cut in flatly. 'And I think the usual written references will do.'

'Lindsay.' The quiet command in his voice stopped her at the door. 'I never actively tried to hide the fact that we were together, I was only trying to protect you from the bitchiness that often occurs when that sort of thing gets out publicly.'

'Thank you,' she said with distaste. 'But after making the decision to move in with you in the first place I certainly wasn't ashamed of it!'

Joel grimaced his impatience. 'Why do you misunderstand or distort everything I say?'

'I don't know,' she shrugged.

He sighed heavily. 'Good luck at your interview.'

She didn't seem to need it when she got to the Robards Advertising Agency later that afternoon, and was seen by the personnel officer first before quickly being passed to Paul Robards himself.

He was a tall fair man in his early fifties, quite good-looking in a world-weary sort of way, his casual but expensive clothes fitting him well, his manner oozing confidence. 'So you work for Joel at the moment?' He looked up from her reference with narrowed eyes.

'Yes,' Lindsay confirmed curtly.

'He writes a glowing report on you, so why do you want to leave?'

It was the usual question for prospective employer to ask, and yet coming from this man, with his lazily assessing blue eyes, she found she didn't like it at all. 'I feel like a change,' she gave him the standard reply.

Blond brows rose. 'In this economic climate?' he queried. 'Surely there has to be more reason than that?'

She didn't like the way he was looking at her; a

cross between speculation and desire. 'No,' she answered abruptly.

He moved around his desk to sit on the edge of it in front of her, one foot swinging backwards and forwards, narrowly eluding touching her thigh as it did so. 'Joel isn't considerate to work for?' he persisted softly.

She moistened suddenly dry lips. 'Mr Sutherland is a very good employer,' she told him curtly.

'But you still want to leave him?'

Lindsay looked up at him sharply, sure this time that she hadn't imagined the innuendo behind his words. 'I want to leave his employment, yes.' She sat awkwardly on the edge of her seat. 'And I was told by the agency that your company was in need of a secretary.'

His gaze was warmly assessing. 'My personal secretary, yes,' he confirmed huskily.

All colour left her cheeks, her glance flickering to the photograph on the desk of his wife and two grown-up children. 'I was under the impression that it was one of the other executives who needed the secretary.'

'Were you?' Paul Robards dismissed uninterestedly. 'But you seem to have all the right qualifications to become my secretary.'

She drew in a ragged breath. 'Mr Robards——'

'Paul, please,' he invited charmingly. 'I feel we could become very good friends.'

That was what she was afraid of! She was sure Joel had kept his word and not telephoned this man, and yet Paul Robards seemed to be well aware of the intimacy of her relationship with Joel in the past. There could be no other possible explanation for his familiar behaviour.

She stood up, moving away from that swinging leg

that somehow made her feel trapped. 'I think there's been some sort of mistake here, Mr Robards——'

'Oh?' His expression darkened, the charm leaving his face as he suddenly looked older, more ruthless.

'I'm leaving Joel's—Mr Sutherland's employment because I want a job with more prospects,' two could play at this double-edged conversation! 'Being your secretary seems to offer the same ones!'

Instead of deflating him as it was meant to her comment brought back the smile to his face. 'Didn't I mention the fact that if you meet my standards, become indispensable to me, there's a possibility of your becoming my personal assistant?' he told her smoothly. 'Not straight away, of course, but——'

'I don't think so, Mr Robards,' she refused stiffly, knowing exactly what 'standards' she would be expected to meet. God, had she become a dirty joke all over London just because she had loved one man enough to live with him? It would seem she had. 'I'm not interested in this job after all,' she told him coldly.

He shrugged. 'The fringe benefits could be highly profitable to an ambitious young woman like you.'

Oh, so now she was being accused of sleeping her way to the top of her career! 'My only ambition at the moment, Mr Robards,' she bit out tautly, 'is to wipe that self-satisfied smirk off your face!' Her eyes flashed dangerously as she looked him up and down with contempt. 'You think you could take Joel's place in my life—in any capacity?' she scorned with a derisive laugh. 'I may be ambitious, but I'm certainly not desperate!'

'Why, you little——'

'Goodbye, Mr Robards,' she told him contemptuously. 'Maybe the next applicant will be interested.' Her tone seemed to imply that she doubted it.

Lindsay was shaking with reaction by the time she got outside, never having met such prejudice before. To think that her actions with Joel had been viewed as ones of ambition and greed rather than love! Well, she couldn't face Joel now, knowing he would ask how the interview had gone. It was already four-thirty, if she didn't go back to the studio he would just assume the interview had gone on longer than expected.

The telephone began ringing about an hour after she got in, and kept on ringing about every fifteen minutes after that. Lindsay lay on the bed in dry-eyed misery, not wanting to talk to anyone right now, not wanting to see anyone either.

But the person ringing the doorbell just after seven o'clock had other ideas, ringing and ringing and ringing until she thought she would go insane.

'Did it ever occur to you that I might have gone out?' she demanded of Joel as she opened the door to find he was her persistent visitor.

'It occurred to me,' he walked past her into the apartment, 'which was why I telephoned Robards before coming over here.'

Her mouth twisted. 'Did you think I would be interested in the "fringe benefits" of being his secretary too?'

His mouth tightened angrily. 'I thought you might have been innocent enough to be taken in by his charm.'

'You knew he was like that?' Her eyes were wide with accusation.

'Unless he's changed drastically in the last few months, yes,' he nodded.

'And you still let me go for an interview with him?'

'It was only a job, Lindsay——'

'As his personal secretary,' she cut in heatedly. 'And

if I made it *very* personal I might even have advanced to being his assistant!'

Joel became suddenly still. He was very casually dressed tonight, his denims close-fitting, resting low down on his hips, his pale yellow shirt partly unbuttoned down his chest. 'Did he say that?' he ground out.

'Yes.' Lindsay was still too stunned and raw from her encounter with Paul Robards to care that the denims and loose shirt she had changed into when she got home were far from glamorous.

'The swine!' Joel bit out forcefully, his eyes glittering angrily. 'Why the hell didn't you come back to the studio after the interview and tell me that? I thought it had gone well, that you might have gone out somewhere to celebrate. What Paul said on the telephone when I talked to him doesn't seem so enigmatic now,' he rasped furiously.

'What did he have to say?' she asked uninterestedly.

'That your qualifications were good, but not good enough,' he muttered with remembered anger. 'I couldn't understand what he meant at the time, your secretarial skills are without fault. And the reference I gave you was excellent.'

Her mouth twisted. 'I believe he may have thought the reference was in regard to something else.'

'He knew about us?' Joel said disbelievingly.

Lindsay gave a jerky nod. 'He spoke as if he did. Oh, he didn't come right out and say it, but he said enough. The two of us are just another dirty joke going about town, Joel.' Her voice was brittle as she put into words what she had realised in Paul Robards' office this afternoon. 'Just another secretary sleeping with her boss to get on in her career.'

'It wasn't like that——'

'How many other couples like us do you think have said the same thing?' she scorned bitterly. 'I've spent the last few hours accepting the facts, Joel, I think you should try and do the same.'

'It wasn't like that between us, Lindsay,' he repeated firmly. 'For one thing, I'm not married, so we're both still free agents, free to choose how we want to live. For another, sleeping with me hardly advanced your career,' he derided. 'If I had to make the decision all over again I know what my choice would be—how about you?' he looked at her with searching eyes.

'The situation will never arise again,' she told him with calm determination, 'because I never intend leaving myself open to that sort of—insult, for a second time.'

He nodded acceptance of the vehemence of her feelings. 'I have no idea how Paul knew about us,' he frowned his puzzlement.

'Maybe he didn't,' she sighed, pushing the short silky curtain of her hair from her face. 'Not specifically. But he did by the time I'd finished telling him he wasn't capable of taking your place in my life—in any capacity,' she recalled with sharp derision.

Humour lightened Joel's eyes to golden. 'Did you mean it?'

Lindsay gave him an impatient look. 'Of course I meant it,' she snapped. 'For a time you were an important part of my life.'

'For a time,' he muttered agreement, as if the thought of them being apart now still didn't please him. 'Have you eaten dinner yet?' he asked suddenly.

Her mouth twisted. 'I've hardly felt like it since I got home. And I'm not in the mood to dress and go out now either,' she added warningly.

'I wasn't going to suggest it,' he taunted, smiling as she blushed. 'However, I do have some culinary skills——'

'Omelettes,' she remembered mockingly.

'As I remember it, you rarely cooked for me either.'

She flushed. 'Maybury was always there to cook your favourite meals—exactly as you liked them.'

'He isn't here now.' Joel raised dark brows challengingly.

'And now I'm not in the mood to cook for you,' she told him without regret.

'Then stop complaining about the omelettes.'

'Joel,' she stopped him at the kitchen door, 'I'm really not hungry.'

'You will be,' he promised lightly, disappearing into her kitchen.

It only took a few minutes of him banging about in her cupboards looking for things before she got up and went in to help him, and the two of them prepared the meal in companionable silence.

'There,' Joel looked at her with satisfaction as she ate the last morsel of cheese they had put out to follow their meal of omelettes and salad. 'Feel better?'

Lindsay felt confused. Now that the food had restored her equilibrium she was wary about what Joel was still doing here. He had satisfied himself as to her wellbeing minutes after being here, now she was wondering why he had lingered to cook her dinner and pour the wine he had found in the fridge to accompany their meal.

'Lindsay?' he prompted, clearing away.

'Why are you doing this, Joel?' She looked at him with wary green eyes.

'Well, I can hardly leave you with all the washing-up,' he deliberately misunderstood her as he filled the sink up with hot water. 'Not after sharing the meal with you.'

'Joel——'

'Take your wine into the other room and sit down,' he ordered firmly. 'I'll join you in a moment.'

To her knowledge domesticity wasn't one of Joel's strong points. She shook her head. 'I'd rather help you.'

He shrugged acceptance, and the two of them did the washing-up together, all the time Lindsay puzzling over how Joel still came to be here. Did he just not have another date this evening and feel at a loose end, or did he have a specific idea for staying here with her? Neither idea particularly pleased her.

'Your wine.' He handed her the glass she had deliberately left in the kitchen when they went through to the lounge, joining her on the sofa.

'Joel——'

'Drink up,' he encouraged softly.

It wasn't the wine that was turning her body to water, it was the thrilling closeness of this man. And she was terrified of the spell he was once again weaving about her, the last week and a half when they had done nothing but snap and snarl at each other fading into the background.

'Joel——'

'I've missed you, Lindsay,' he groaned throatily, pulling her into his arms after putting their wine glasses down on the table in front of them. 'I never knew my bed was so big until it no longer had you in it.'

And she hadn't realised how long the nights were until she no longer had him to share them with! She knew she had spoken the words out loud as Joel gave a satisfied groan before claiming her lips in a kiss that shook her to the roots of her being.

It was no chaste, exploratory kiss, their relationship having progressed past that long ago; Lindsay's mouth parted beneath his, the warmth of Joel's tongue thrusting deeply into the dark warm cavern beneath. It was as if she had been physically claimed in that moment, with Joel's hands on her spine as he moulded her to him, the thrust of her breasts warm against him, the nipples already taut.

'Ah, Lindsay,' he moaned raggedly as he buried his face in her throat, his body shaking against hers.

It had been much too long for both of them, and emotions were quickly spiralling out of control, Lindsay gasping as Joel's hand moved deftly beneath her loose shirt to capture her breast, his thumb flicking over her turgid nipple, the trembling of her body accompanied by a pleasurable ache that began at the centre of the warm moistness of her womanhood and spread quickly through the rest of her body.

'Let me look at you.' His eyes were dark with emotion as he gazed down at her, his hands slightly unsteady as he undid the buttons to her shirt, smoothing the material back to her shoulders, her breasts small but pert, the nipples deeply engorged and raised to his heated gaze. 'You're so beautiful, Lindsay.' He buried his face against her breasts, kissing each satiny inch, prolonging the moment when he would take the nipple fully into the moistness of his mouth.

But before he could reach that intimacy the telephone began to ring, startling Lindsay out of the sensual haze she had fallen into, although Joel was slower to return to an awareness of their surroundings, his arms tightening about her momentarily before he reluctantly released her, his face flushed with desire.

'The telephone must be the most sadistic appliance

ever invented,' he muttered as he watched her move to answer the call. 'It must ruin more romantic moments than anything else!'

Lindsay's hands shook as she rebuttoned her shirt, not answering him as she picked up the telephone receiver. There had been nothing in the least *romantic* about what had just happened between them, they had just wanted each other with near desperation.

'Lindsay?' Malcolm queried as she recited her telephone number completely wrong.

'I—oh—sorry,' she said in a flustered voice, aware of Joel's narrow-eyed gaze on her. 'How are you?'

'Great. Just great,' he told her in a pleased voice. 'I'm just on my way to pick up Judi for our first date, and I thought I would tell you the good news.'

'I'm pleased for you!' She had difficulty concentrating even on such good news with Joel staring at her in that brooding way! 'Er—I mustn't keep you,' she added breathlessly as Joel stood up and began to unbutton his shirt.

'Lindsay, are you all right?' Malcolm sounded worried. 'You seem a little—agitated.'

Agitated wasn't the word for how she felt as Joel took off his shirt completely, his hands going to the belt on his denims. 'I'm fine. Really,' she added in a choked voice as Joel went through the torturously slow process of unfastening the belt. 'You got me out of the bath,' she added desperately.

'I'm sorry about that,' Malcolm chuckled. 'Judi will probably call you and let you know how we got on.'

'Probably.' She spoke between clenched teeth as Joel came up behind her to cup her breasts, his face in her hair, his arousal pressed into the back of her thighs.

'And then I'll call you and find out what she said,' added Malcolm with satisfaction.

'All right. I—Oh!' she groaned as the moist warmth of Joel's probing tongue hungrily outlined her ear. 'I have to go,' she told Malcolm hastily. 'I—I'm getting cold.'

'Cold?' Joel laughed softly after she had hung up. 'I thought it was the opposite!'

'It is,' she shivered pleasurably as she turned into his arms. 'And what you just did wasn't fair.'

'I enjoyed it,' he said with devilment, knowing she had too. 'Who was that on the phone?'

'Just a friend,' she dismissed, loath to break the spell of the moment, knowing she needed him very badly. 'I thought I was going to collapse when you started your strip-tease act,' she grimaced her discomfort.

'I just didn't want our romantic interlude interrupted by a telephone call. But I didn't want to take all my clothes off myself.' He paused. 'I much prefer it when you undress me.'

Lindsay preferred it too, loved to caress every hard plane and contour of his body, just as she was doing now to his broad back and chest. 'You're a devil, Joel,' she groaned.

'I know,' he was unperturbed by the accusation. 'But you are going to let me stay here tonight, aren't you.'

It wasn't a question but a statement, and she knew she couldn't let him leave her now, that she wanted him too much. Her face was raised invitingly to his to give him her answer.

CHAPTER SIX

JOEL eagerly accepted that invitation, his mouth closing possessively over hers, one of his hands between them as he deftly undid the buttons on her shirt for a second time, their bare torsos meeting with searing heat.

It felt good, so good, like food after years of famine, and Lindsay feasted on his mouth even as he did the same to hers, her tongue teasing his lips in a way that she knew he found exciting.

His hands were on her hips now, pulling her into him, devastating her with the hardness of his thighs as he moved sensuously against her, even as his mouth moved warm and deep on hers. 'I need this, Lindsay,' he told her raggedly between kisses. 'Tell me you need it too.'

'I need you.' Her words were unconsciously more personal than his.

His gaze was warm on her parted lips. 'Then I'm waiting.'

She blinked to try and clear the sexual haze and understand what he meant. 'For what?'

'To be invited to your bed,' he teased her gently. 'I've always invited you to mine in the past.'

It was true, Joel had never shared her bed, only she his. 'It's through there,' she nodded towards her bedroom.

'I want the words, Lindsay.'

She swallowed hard. 'You want me to beg?'

'No,' he groaned, 'not that. I just want you to

need me enough to ask.'

It wasn't that much to ask when it must be perfectly obvious that she was going out of her mind with wanting him! 'Come to bed with me, Joel,' she invited softly. 'Make love with me.'

He shuddered his reaction, his eyes dark with desire. 'This will be my welcome home from America,' he told her raggedly. 'The one I envisaged for us.'

There was no condemnation in his voice, just disappointment that he had come back to find her gone. Lindsay was glad he couldn't know what it had cost her to *be* gone.

They left the room in darkness as they closed the door behind them, light shining in from the street outside. Lindsay didn't hesitate, moving across the room to finish what Joel had started when she was on the telephone with Malcolm, easing the tightness of his denims down over his aroused manhood, revealing the expected pair of dark briefs. Joel had a drawerfull of such briefs, all them in navy, black, or dark brown. They were black tonight, and Lindsay removed them with the minimum of effort, her hands gently caressing the hardness of him as she knelt in front of him.

'My turn,' Joel's voice was hoarse as he pulled her to her feet. 'I've had such fantasies about you, Lindsay!'

She had had plenty of dreams about him herself, most of them leaving her bathed in perspiration as she longed for the reality of those dreams.

She stood perfectly still as his lean hands slowly pushed her shirt down her arms to fall on the carpeted floor, those same hands moving to cup her pert breasts, loving the firm weight of them as he bent his head to suckle first one nipple and then the other, while needles of pleasure coursed through her body.

He fell to his knees in front of her, unzipping the denims to kiss the heated flesh he bared as he discarded them on top of her shirt, her only clothing now a pair of black lace briefs. Her whimpers were ones of desperate need as she felt his hands move beneath the fabric to cup her bottom and pull her closer into him.

Joel knew exactly what he was doing, he had introduced her to the erotic pleasure of wearing such underwear when he bought her a red camisole and matching lace bikini briefs, giving them both pleasure unimaginable as he slowly removed them.

He didn't have quite the same control tonight, ripping the black lace slightly as he pulled the briefs from her body, his hands on her hips bent her into him.

'Joel . . .!' she gasped weakly at the pleasure she felt, clasping on to his shoulders for support.

'I want you like this, Lindsay,' he rasped raggedly. 'I want to feel you as you explode.'

She wasn't far from doing that now, her body finely attuned to every caress of his lips and tongue, collapsing against him as his hands moved to capture her breasts, rolling the nipples between his thumb and finger until he felt the spasms that rocked her body and her moistness explode around him, falling to the floor in front of him as he buried his face in her throat.

'Oh, Lindsay, Lindsay,' he told her shakily. 'I can't get enough of you.'

But it was ner turn to take control now, pushing him back on the deep-pile carpet, holding him captive with her hands while her lips slowly travelled across his chest, savouring first one male nipple and then the other as he groaned the pleasure that she gave him. Her tongue moved lower, dipping moistly into his navel.

'Stop now, Lindsay,' he pleaded raggedly. 'I can't take much more!'

She didn't intend him to, continuing her caresses until he lay replete beneath her, his eyes like molten gold as he looked at her in wonder, his breathing slowly steadying to normal.

'Lindsay——'

She snuggled against his shoulder. 'We still haven't shared my bed,' she teased, not willing to discuss the intimacy of the lovemaking they had just shared. Always in the past Joel had caressed her to such a fever-pitch of desire and longing that she hadn't cared what he did with her, but never before had he let her take that initiative with him, always stopping her before he lost control. Tonight she had been determined he wouldn't be able to do that, had known as the first spasm of ecstasy shot through his body that she had succeeded. For that moment Joel had been hers completely, and she intended for him to remain that way at least until morning.

'I don't know if I have the strength to get up,' he told her self-derisively.

'Then we can just stay here.' She kissed the firmness of his jaw, giving it loving little nibbles.

'Oh no, you don't, young lady!' He held her back from him, getting to his feet to pull her up beside him. 'If this is the effect absence has on you I'll have to go away more often!'

As they lay down on the bed together Lindsay knew he was still playing the game, imagining he had just returned from New York, that the bitterness of the last two weeks hadn't happened. She preferred it that way too; she didn't want to think of the emotional consequences of what they were doing. When morning came would be time enough to regret her actions, morning always seemed to bring with it regret.

'If you had taken me with you we could have had this every night,' she teased, half serious, wishing he had never given her the time to decide to leave him.

'I wanted to ask you to join me out there, Lindsay,' Joel told her seriously.

'Then why didn't you?' she frowned.

His arms tightened about her. 'I wish to God I had, maybe then you——'

Her fingertips over his lips silenced him. 'This is your first night back, Joel, let's not waste any of it.'

For a brief moment he seemed lost to her, his thoughts tortuous, and then he shook off the darkness of those thoughts, his eyes turning to gold once more. 'No, let's not waste any of it,' he said fiercely, kissing her savagely, quickly arousing her once again.

There was no gentleness in either of them as his body thrust into her waiting one, pausing for a moment to savour the pleasure of their joining, then moving quickly inside her, Lindsay meeting each thrust with one of her own, the two of them crying out their satisfaction in unison.

'I think you should rest now.' Joel held her firmly against him as they lay exhausted in each other's arms. 'You're going to need your strength later.'

Joel hadn't exaggerated, waking her time and time again during the night as he made love to her with a fierceness that bordered on desperation. Lindsay finally woke alone to the smell of fresh coffee percolating. She stretched languorously, relieved that Joel was still there, her body a pleasurable ache, every part of her fulfilled, turning to smile at Joel as he brought her in a cup of the coffee.

'Drink it while it's hot.' He put the coffee down on the side table next to her, his words spoken lightly enough, although there was a wary look in his eyes as he sat on the bed beside her.

Lindsay could understand that wariness; she was a little unsure herself where they went from here, or if indeed they went anywhere. 'You're up early.' She sipped the coffee, unselfconscious about her nakedness as she sat up in the bed.

'It's eight-thirty,' he mocked. 'And I still have to go home and change my clothes,' he derided the casual clothes he wore.

'I'm sure your secretary will cover for you.' She kept up the lightness, not knowing how else to cope with this situation.

'Lindsay——'

'This coffee is good, Joel.'

'Lindsay, we have to talk——'

'No, we don't,' she dismissed brittly, pushing back the bedclothes to get out of bed, her body a warm honey colour, her hair silky despite being dishevelled.

'Last night—God, I've bruised you!' His eyes were dark as he stood up to touch the darkened skin on her hip.

She shrugged. 'I'm seem to remember I scratched your back, so we're even.'

'Lindsay, for God's sake take this seriously,' he rasped. 'How do you feel about last night?'

'Satisfied,' she drawled, reluctant to hear what

their future would be now that it had come to the crunch.

His expression darkened. 'That's all?'

'Isn't it enough?' she mocked.

A pulse moved erratically in his jaw as she faced him with proud nakedness, her breasts thrusting firmly, her stomach taut and flat, her thighs warm and inviting. 'It's enough for now,' groaned Joel raggedly, taking her in his arms once more. 'It's more than enough for now!'

The night they had just spent together hadn't dulled his desire for her at all, and by the time he left her bed half an hour later she was the one who lay weak with exhaustion.

Joel dressed hurriedly. 'I have to go,' he told her regretfully. 'I have an important appointment this morning. Come in later if you feel like it,' he said indulgently. 'We'll talk then.'

Lindsay was hardly aware of him leaving as she began to doze, never having known Joel to be as demanding a lover as this even during the six months they had lived together.

Joel had seemed different last night, more willing to share even his sexual pleasure, not denying her any intimacy. And he was the one who wanted to talk. It gave her hope, a faint hope she clung to as she showered, dressed and went to the studio.

Everything there seemed to be the same as it had when she left yesterday, but somehow she had changed, in a very tangible way. Surely Joel couldn't have made love to her the way he had if he still felt nothing for her? She couldn't believe even he was capable of that!

He was in the middle of a photographic session when she arrived and settled down to work, but she knew they would have the opportunity to talk later.

She wasn't prepared for the shock that awaited her, and was standing at the filing cabinet when the outside door opened, the potent perfume reaching her before she turned and saw the woman herself. The woman's figure would have been thought boyish in the black silk trouser suit if it weren't for the fact that her bust bordered on the voluptuous, the low vee-neckline of the loose top showing that she wore nothing beneath. The hair was as black and long as ever, the green eyes surrounded by thick sooty lashes, the creamy complexion highlighted by blusher on the high cheekbones, a deep plum-coloured lipgloss outlining the pouting lips. Lindsay would recognise the other woman anywhere—Marilyn Mills!

All sorts of thoughts became jumbled in her mind. Did Joel know this woman was coming here today? Could it be that Marilyn Mills was his 'important appointment'? She certainly didn't think any of the other people he was to see this morning fitted the bill. Last, and worst of all, had the other woman coming here today influenced Joel into staying one more night with *her*? It was this last possibility that disturbed her, and her defences crumbled as she took in the haunting loveliness of the other woman. No wonder Joel had never been able to forget her!

Well, he seemed to have kept to his word and 'taken care' of the problem of the other woman quite effectively. Lindsay seemed to be the one with a problem now; where did she stand in all this? She didn't have time to answer her own question. Marilyn Mills walked gracefully across the room to look at her expectantly.

'I have an appointment to see Joel,' she said

impatiently when Lindsay still seemed to be struck dumb seconds later, her accent surprisingly English when Lindsay had been expecting her to be an American.

She moistened dry lips, hoping her voice would come out normally when she did speak. 'For what time?' Her tone was as haughty as the other woman's, already knowing that she didn't have an appointment written down in the book for Marilyn Mills.

Green eyes met similar eyes the colour of emeralds as the model looked down at her contemptuously. 'For any time I cared to get here,' she drawled. 'Just tell Joel I've arrived, he'll see me,' she dismissed with arrogance.

Lindsay hadn't liked the other woman before she met her, hated the significance she had in Joel's life, but now that she had actually met the beautiful model she disliked her even more, not liking her attitude one little bit.

She moved slowly across the room to sit behind her desk, instantly putting the other girl at a disadvantage, taking her time about looking through Joel's appointment book. 'You really should have made an appointment, Miss——?' She looked up questioningly, having no intention of letting this woman know that she knew exactly who she was.

'Mills,' the other woman rasped, her mouth tight. 'Marilyn Mills,' she said her name as if Lindsay should have known it. 'And if you'll just tell Joel that I'm here——'

'I'm afraid I can't do that.' Lindsay shook her head, being deliberately obstructive. 'Joel hates to be disturbed when he's in the middle of a photographic session,' she emphasised the word hates, knowing as the other girl's mouth set resignedly that she was well aware of Joel's temper when roused.

'Very well,' Marilyn Mills snapped, 'I'll wait. But I can assure you that you will be the one who's disturbed him when he knows how you've kept me waiting out here!'

Lindsay had a feeling the other woman could be right about that, but the perverse satisfaction of making her wait persisted, was even worth risking Joel's temper for.

The model sat down in one of the plush black leather armchairs that faced Lindsay, taking a long cigarette holder from her clutch-bag before lighting up a cigarette with a matching gold lighter. 'How long have you been sitting guard over Joel?' She made the question sound insulting.

'I've been his secretary for a little over a year,' Lindsay answered tightly.

Green eyes narrowed speculatively. 'You're certainly an improvement on the last old battleaxe he had working for him,' she drawled.

'Mrs Greg retired,' Lindsay said stiffly.

'I'm not surprised,' Marilyn Mills mocked lightly. 'She was ancient seven years ago!'

'I believe Mrs Greg was fifty-five when she retired last year.'

'Like I said, she was ancient,' the model dismissed cruelly. 'Whereas you are surprisingly young.' Her eyes narrowed thoughtfully on Lindsay's slender beauty. 'What happened, couldn't you make it as a model and decided to settle for second best?'

Lindsay mentally counted to ten to prevent the explosive retort she wanted to make to the deliberately insulting comment. 'I never take second best, Miss Mills,' she told the other woman with quiet forcefulness. 'I work as Joel's secretary because I enjoy doing it. The career of a model has never appealed to me—it's too false and too demanding.'

The beautiful mouth twisted mockingly. 'And isn't being Joel's—secretary demanding?'

She stiffened warily, looking at the other girl searchingly. Had she given herself away with her defensive attitude? Possibly, but why should she care? Any hopes that might have resurfaced because of last night had been dashed the moment this woman arrived at the studio. She had nothing more to lose. 'It has been,' she answered abruptly. 'But I've learnt to cope with it.'

'I just bet you have!' Marilyn Mills stubbed the cigarette out viciously in the ashtray, standing up. 'Look, I don't care who Joel has in there with him, I want to see him now. Do you understand——' She broke off as the studio door opened unexpectedly and Joel appeared to show the model out.

It was as if Joel was aware of Marilyn Mills' presence in the room even before he had turned and seen her, the tension in his body increasing as his face paled. Colette Gates was forgotten as he stared at the beautiful dark-haired woman who stood across the room from him, and Lindsay felt sure he had forgotten her presence too. Her heart ached at his reaction to Marilyn Mills, looking almost as if he had seen a vision, a ghost, perhaps even his nemesis. Whatever had happened to separate them in the past, Joel was more deeply affected by Marilyn Mills than he had been by any other woman, including Lindsay. And she knew it.

'Joel!' Marilyn Mills purred softly, moving across the room to twine her arms about his neck and raise her face invitingly for his kiss. When he seemed too numbed to take the initiative she pressed her lips against his in a slow leisurely kiss. 'Darling, it's so good to see you,' she murmured throatily.

Joel's breathing was uneven when she moved back slightly, his face more haggard than ever. 'I had no idea you had arrived yet,' his voice lacked its usual self-confidence.

She glanced maliciously at Lindsay. 'Your secretary was very——unco-operative, sweet,' she purred.

Joel looked at Lindsay as if he had only just noticed her presence, an expression akin to pleading in his eyes, whether for understanding or something else she didn't know. 'Lindsay knows I don't like to be disturbed when I'm working,' he defended, although it seemed to Lindsay that his voice lacked conviction.

Long scarlet-tipped fingers caressed the rigidness of his jaw. 'And would I have disturbed you, darling?'

Joel seemed at a loss how to answer, and Lindsay's protective instinct sprang into action, no matter how much he might have hurt her by using her last night. 'I'm sorry if I should have shown Miss Mills straight in, Joel,' she told him softly. 'I had no idea the two of you were such good friends,' she couldn't resist adding challengingly.

'For years and years,' the other woman told her with throaty satisfaction, her body still pressed seductively against Joel's. 'Now let's go through to the studio, darling,' she encouraged huskily, 'and you can tell me all the news. How are your parents?' Lindsay heard her asking as the door to the studio was firmly closed behind them.

Lindsay felt the tears come into her eyes unbidden, choked with emotion that the other woman had actually met Joel's parents during their relationship when he had never even spoken of them to her! Now

she knew what last night had all been about—farewell
to his new mistress before he took back his old one!
God, it was so humiliating to think that she had held
such high hopes about last night, felt closer to Joel
then than at any time when she had lived with him.
Would he compare last night with tonight when he
slept with Marilyn? Because she had no doubt they
would be sleeping together tonight. Would he confirm
for the other woman what she had already guessed,
that she had been much more than his secretary in the
past, that she had inflicted the scratch and bite marks
he wouldn't be able to hide? Somehow she didn't
think even that would convince the other girl that she
was much of a threat to her renewed relationship with
him.

And neither did Lindsay. She had never seen Joel
like this before, stunned and completely speechless,
his emotions in his eyes for all to see. If Marilyn Mills
had been the one to sour him against love she was also
the one to bring it back into his life. Joel had at last
fallen in love, and with another woman.

Indeed, when he and the model left for lunch ten
minutes later he still seemed dazed, making no
mention of when, or if, he would be back, and if he
wasn't what Lindsay should do about his afternoon
appointments.

Now that she was alone Lindsay allowed the tears
to fall, her head buried in her arms as she saw the man
she loved so captivated by another. And she didn't like
the other woman. And that wasn't just because of
Joel's reaction to her, she genuinely didn't like
Marilyn Mills' hard beauty or brittle manner.

'Sleeping on the job?' teased a lightly mocking voice
that she instantly recognised.

She looked up with a start at Malcolm finding her

like this, her make-up streaked from the tears she had just shed, her distress obvious.

Malcolm's humour instantly changed to concern. 'Lindsay, what is it?'

'Nothing.' She hastily wiped the evidence of tears from her face with a tissue.

'Hey, this is your future brother-in-law you're talking to,' he chided softly.

That brought a watery smile to her lips, as it was supposed to. 'You're very confident,' she teased.

'Hopeful,' he dismissed, his face still dark with concern. 'Did Joel do this to you?' His voice hardened.

'He didn't do a thing,' she sniffed, standing up to check her appearance in the mirror, her eyes red from the crying she had done, her make-up more or less washed away.

'You weren't crying for nothing,' Malcolm persisted.

'We women do, you know,' she dismissed, setting about the repairing of her make-up.

'Not you,' he shook his head. 'You're a very together young lady.'

Lindsay grimaced. 'And I just fell apart.' Her eyes looked a little less grotesque now, her brown shadow and mascara nearly reapplied. 'How did your date with Judi go last night?' she changed the subject without answering his questions.

'She hasn't called you?' Malcolm looked disappointed.

'Not yet,' she smiled. 'Although I'm sure she will.'

'It went surprisingly well,' he told her in pleased voice. 'We didn't argue once.'

Her brows rose. 'Then it did go well,' she teased.

He nodded. 'She's agreed to see me tonight too.'

'The Reader charm must be working,' Lindsay smiled again.

'I wish it would work on you.' He watched her with narrowed eyes. 'I wish you would open up and talk to me. You seemed a little strange on the telephone last night too,' he remembered thoughtfully.

'I wasn't strange,' she dismissed, a delicate blush colouring her cheeks. 'I was getting cold standing there talking to you.'

'Were you really in the bath when I telephoned?' he asked with slow scepticism.

Lindsay blushed even more. 'Of course. Why would I lie about something like that?'

'You tell me,' he shrugged. 'You didn't sound like someone freezing to death. I—Oh hello, Joel,' he greeted the other man lightly as he had stood unobserved in the doorway.

Lindsay turned sharply from the mirror, her lipgloss still in her hand, knowing by the hard glitter of Joel's eyes that he had completely misunderstood the situation and the conversation. Her flushed face and bare lips gave the impression that she had just been thoroughly kissed, and she had no idea how much of the conversation he had overheard, but it seemed to be enough for him to have misconstrued the significance of the telephone call she had received from her 'friend' Malcolm the previous evening.

But who was he to sit in judgment, even if what he believed was true? His motives for spending the night with her were even more reprehensible!

Her chin rose challengingly. 'I thought you'd gone to lunch, Joel,' she said tautly.

'Obviously.' His mouth twisted as he looked pointedly at the other man. 'I forgot something in the studio,' he explained his unexpected return. 'I didn't expect to see you here today, Malcolm.' He looked questioningly at the other man.

Malcolm grinned, perfectly relaxed. 'I just can't seem to keep away from your beautiful secretary.'

His words were meant to be provocative, and Lindsay could see by Joel's taut expression that they had succeeded.

'So I see,' he bit out curtly. 'Well, do you think you could tear yourself away from her long enough to join me for lunch? Marilyn Mills has arrived from the States, I'm sure you'd enjoy talking to her.'

A light of interest brightened Malcolm's eyes. 'I'm sure I would, but unfortunately I have other plans for lunch.' He didn't enlarge on that statement, although it was obvious from the way he looked at Lindsay that she was included in those plans. 'Maybe I could meet her later in the afternoon,' he suggested smoothly. 'After lunch.'

Joel looked far from pleased. 'If that's what you would prefer,' his voice echoed his displeasure. 'I'll just go into the studio for a few minutes and then leave you to your own plans.'

As soon as they were alone Lindsay turned to the other man. 'Malcolm, what do you——'

'Ssh!' he told her fiercely as Joel came back from the studio, giving the other man a bright smile. 'See you later, Joel,' he said provocatively.

'Yes,' Joel acknowledged tersely, and closed the door behind him with force.

CHAPTER SEVEN

'WHAT did you do that for?' Lindsay demanded irritably as soon as the door closed.

Malcolm gave her an innocent look. 'Do what?'

'You know very well what,' she sighed. 'Don't you think things are bad enough between Joel and me without you coming along with a big wooden spoon and stirring it some more?'

He laughed softly. 'I just love your crazy English sayings!'

'Don't come the wide-eyed American tourist with me, Malcolm Reader,' she snapped her impatience. 'You deliberately antagonised Joel just now, and you know it.'

Malcolm shrugged. 'He didn't look as if he needed much pushing.'

'Perhaps not,' she acknowledged grudgingly. 'But you had to push anyway, didn't you?'

'All I did was say I had other plans for lunch——'

'Implying that I was included in them!'

'Well, you are, why else do you think I turned up here at lunchtime?'

'To gloat over how my poor sister is being taken in by your charm,' she derided.

'That too,' he grinned. 'But I also thought I could take you out to lunch.'

Lindsay shrugged. 'You heard Joel, he's taken Miss Mills out; I'm not expecting him back for a couple of hours at least.' If then!

'All the more reason for you to go to lunch yourself,'

Malcolm dismissed. 'Put the answering machine on, lock the door, and let's go. You have a right to eat, Lindsay,' he encouraged as she still hesitated.

He was right, of course, and if Joel took the couple of hours she thought he would then it was going to be too late for her to go to lunch when he returned. Besides, he must have realised she was going to be out of the office at the same time as he was, and he hadn't raised any objections. 'All right,' she agreed, doing as Malcolm suggested before following him down to his car.

As was usually the case in restaurants in town at lunchtime during the week it was very busy, but they managed to find a table in a quietly exclusive one in a side street, relaxing after they had ordered their meal.

'So what happened this morning to upset you?' Malcolm persisted remorselessly.

'I told you,' Lindsay's tone was light, 'women often cry for no real reason.'

'And would this "no real reason" have anything to do with the arrival of Marilyn Mills?' he asked shrewdly.

She blushed slightly. 'Of course not——'

'Lindsay, I meant it when I said I'm going to be your brother-in-law,' he told her seriously. 'And as such I'm concerned for you. I should have realised by Joel's reaction to having Marilyn Mills for "Witchcraft" that he once had something going with her. He did, didn't he?'

She swallowed hard, moistening her lips. 'I—I think so,' she nodded. 'He hasn't actually said so, but like you I found his reaction a little—surprising.'

'And he's taken her out to lunch now,' Malcolm said thoughtfully.

'That's nothing unusual,' she excused. 'He often takes his models out to lunch.'

'And do you always react this way when he does?' he derided disbelievingly.

'Malcolm, I told you——'

'What's she like?' he interrupted sharply, looking at her with narrowed eyes.

Lindsay's expression became shuttered. 'Beautiful. Even more so than her photographs, if that's possible.'

'That wasn't what I meant and you know it,' Malcolm said dryly. 'What's she like as a person?'

'I didn't see her long enough to——'

'Lindsay,' he rebuked softly, 'it usually only takes a couple of minutes to form an opinion of someone.'

'I could be biased——'

'So give me your biased opinion of her,' he mocked.

She shrugged. 'I didn't like her,' she told him quietly. 'And I'm sure the feeling was mutual.'

'She guessed about you and Joel, hm?' he said dryly.

Lindsay blushed a deep red as she remembered the night she and Joel had just shared. 'There's nothing to guess any more——'

'Lindsay,' Malcolm questioned slowly, 'when I called you last night did I interrupt something?'

It would have been so easy to lie, to have prevaricated, but she did neither. 'Only temporarily,' she answered steadily.

His expression darkened. 'And after spending the night with you Joel has calmly gone off with an old lover?'

'Yes.'

'When I first met you I thought the man was a fool for not claiming you for his own, but once I realised that he had I began to think he had some sense after all. But to go straight from your arms to Marilyn Mills——!'

'Don't you think that now you could be acting a little biased?—as my future brother-in-law, of course,' she derided dryly.

'If I hadn't fallen for Judi the moment I saw her I'd still be after you myself. Joel's a fool to let a past love ruin what he has now,' he frowned darkly.

'He doesn't have anything with me now,' Lindsay dismissed brittly. 'Last night was—a mistake.'

Malcolm shook his head. 'You aren't the type to make mistakes like that.'

'Maybe not, but Joel does.' She turned to smile at the waiter as he brought their meal. 'Let's just enjoy the food, hm?' she prompted once they were alone.

Malcolm nodded, sensing her need not to discuss Joel any more for the moment, telling her instead about the previous evening he had spent with Judi. It did indeed sound as if her sister had mellowed towards him, and Lindsay could only hope it would continue that way. It didn't seem as if Judi had confided in Malcolm about Jonathan yet, and until she did that it meant she didn't completely trust him.

Joel and Marilyn Mills hadn't returned by the time they did, so Malcolm sat down to wait for them while Lindsay caught up on her work. Marilyn Mills' husky laugh preceded them into the office, the other woman clinging to Joel's arm as they entered the room together, her green eyes gleaming with the satisfaction of a cat as she looked triumphantly at Lindsay, those same eyes widening with interest as she spotted Malcolm.

Lindsay had no interest in the other woman's cattiness; her gaze was set on Joel, his expression coldly dismissive as he looked right back at her. They were completely back to the daggers being drawn that had existed between them since his return from America, it was just as if last night had never happened.

Maybe it never had, not in the way she wanted it to anyway. It never would again, of that she was sure.

She watched uninterestedly as Joel tersely made the introductions between the other two, Malcolm's expression one of amusement as the model flirted with him provocatively. Whether Marilyn Mills was trying to make Joel jealous, or if she just came on that way with every man she met, Lindsay had no idea. She did know that Joel looked far from pleased by the exchange. Perhaps he had finally met the woman he couldn't control or dominate; it certainly seemed like it. That might even have had something to do with their break-up seven years ago.

Malcolm turned to give Lindsay an outrageously suggestive wink as the three of them went into the studio, and Lindsay's mood at once lightened. Malcolm for one didn't appear to be taken in by Marilyn Mills' softly purring voice, even found the situation funny enough to make a joke of it. Joel obviously didn't feel the same way about the other woman.

She could hear the murmur of voices in the adjoining room for the next half hour, looking up warily as the door finally opened, then relaxing slightly as Malcolm came out alone.

He came over to lean across her desk. 'I don't like her either,' he said softly.

'Now who's being unfair?' she mocked.

He shook his head. 'The woman is a barracuda. She eats men up and spits them out again.'

Lindsay laughed softly at the description. 'Isn't that a little strong?'

'I don't think so.' He shuddered with distaste. 'Not my type *at all*.'

'Come on,' Lindsay teased, although she was secretly pleased he didn't like the other girl either. 'Miss Mills is every man's type!'

'Not mine,' he said seriously. 'Although she's going to be perfect for "Witchcraft".'

'You've definitely decided on her, then?' Her voice was deliberately casual.

He grimaced. 'I think *she* made the decision,' he derided. 'But I'm quite happy to go along with it. At least, I would be,' he frowned, 'if it didn't mean you were going to be hurt even more.'

'Oh, don't worry about me,' she dismissed with a bravado she was far from feeling. 'I think I can stand it for the short time I have left here.'

Malcolm's frown deepened. 'What do you mean?'

'I only have a little over two weeks to go before I leave, so I——'

'You've handed in your resignation?' He sounded astounded. 'And Joel accepted it?' he demanded disgustedly once she had nodded her head in confirmation.

'He could hardly do anything else,' she said dryly.

'There were plenty of other things he could have done—ripped the damn thing up and pretended he had never seen it for one!'

Lindsay shrugged. 'It wouldn't have done any good, I would have just written another one.'

'Then he doesn't actually want you to leave?' Malcolm pounced on the fact that she hadn't denied that.

She refused to meet his gaze. 'I didn't give him a choice,' she said quietly.

'I wish there was something I could do to sort you two out,' he told her regretfully.

'We don't need "sorting out",' she chided. 'And don't you have enough to do convincing my sister you're irresistible?'

'She already knows I am,' he grinned. 'She just won't admit it yet.'

Lindsay shook her head ruefully. 'And they say women are the conceited ones!'

After the playful banter she had shared with Malcolm she was very tense as she waited for Marilyn Mills to leave and the expected confrontation with Joel. He wasn't going to let what he thought he saw and heard between her and Malcolm earlier pass without comment, she felt sure of that.

As she had known he would, Joel walked the other woman to the entrance door, Marilyn Mills somehow managing to look small and kittenish next to him despite her height and obvious self-assurance, once again clinging to Joel's arm as she gazed up at him adoringly, both of them ignoring Lindsay's presence in the room as they said their goodbyes for now.

'You'll call me?' Marilyn Mills prompted throatily.

'Yes,' Joel confirmed abruptly.

'I'm at the Hilton.'

'I know,' he nodded.

'Of course you do,' she said with satisfaction. 'I'll look forward to seeing you later.' Her hand caressed his jaw as she kissed him lingeringly on the mouth, then turned to Lindsay with challenging green eyes. 'So nice to have met you,' she said with an obvious lack of sincerity.

Lindsay didn't bother to answer, merely nodded acknowledgement of the other woman, knowing that anything she said would sound just as insincere.

Joel turned sharply back into the room once the beautiful model had left, his expression cold as he walked past Lindsay's desk. Suddenly he stopped and turned back to her. 'So it was only a "friend" who telephoned you last night!' he rasped accusingly.

She had been thrown temporarily off guard by the fact that he seemed to be going back into the studio without speaking to her, taking several seconds to collect herself enough to answer him calmly. 'That's right,' she nodded. 'A friend.'

'A friend that turned up here today and kissed you almost senseless!' His eyes glittered icily.

'That isn't——'

'I wonder what he would have said if he'd known that last night all your kisses belonged to me,' Joel bit out insultingly.

Lindsay sighed resignedly. 'Malcolm knows about last night,' she told him dully.

His eyes narrowed. 'You told him I stayed with you?' He sounded disbelieving.

'I didn't have to, he guessed.'

'Guessed?' Joel echoed sceptically. 'How the hell do you *guess* a thing like that?'

She shrugged. 'He just did.'

'And you admitted it was true?'

She looked up at him with unflinching green eyes. 'I've never believed in lying about our relationship, Joel, you know that.'

'Did he know when he came into the studio just now with Marilyn and me?' he asked slowly.

'Yes.'

'And he still managed to be polite?' Joel said disbelievingly. 'If it had been me——' he broke off with an angry sigh.

'Yes?' she prompted softly.

He shook his head dismissively. 'That's some relationship you and he have.'

Lindsay still didn't flinch at his derisive tone. 'It's based on trust and understanding, Joel, things you know nothing about.'

'Trust and understanding,' he repeated scathingly. 'When he knows damn well you spent the night with another man! What warped sort of trust is that?'

'The trust between two people who care for each other, who understand that each of them is fallible, and don't judge because they are. But at least I don't leave my bed with one man and calmly go into the arms of another,' she added pointedly.

His eyes were a dark tempestuous tawny gold. 'It looked that way to me.'

'Looks can be deceiving. Although the same can't be said for you, can it?'

'Implying?'

She shrugged. 'You didn't exactly try to hide your behaviour with Miss Mills.'

'*My* behaviour?' he repeated incredulously. 'I never touched the woman!'

Lindsay flushed angrily. 'But you didn't object when *she* touched *you*!'

'Marilyn is like that with all men,' he rasped. 'It doesn't mean a damned thing.'

'It meant something to me!' Her control finally broke. 'You left my bed only this morning after a night when—Well, I don't ever remember it being that—passionate, between us before. And only hours later you're letting another woman paw you as if no other women exist!'

'Lindsay——'

'You didn't even confide in me that she was coming here,' she continued accusingly. 'I just had to wait until she walked in and claimed you. So much for that talk, hm, Joel?' she jeered bitterly. 'I don't think it's necessary now, do you?'

He sighed raggedly. 'You don't understand——'

'No, it's you who doesn't understand,' she told him heatedly. 'No matter what opinion you may have of me, Joel, I didn't take last night lightly. I know you can't love me, you've always made that clear, but I thought that I at least meant a little more to you than a one-night stand!'

He was very pale. 'It wasn't like that——'

'Oh, but it was,' she choked. 'Because you can believe it will never happen again.'

'Lindsay, for God's sake let me at least explain about Marilyn. She——'

'It's too late for explanations, Joel,' she told him hardly. 'Much too late. Just stay away from me now until I leave here.'

'You really mean that?' he asked huskily.

'God, yes, I mean it,' she choked. 'When I think what I allowed to happen last night I feel ill!'

He swallowed convulsively, his expression tight. 'I'm sorry you feel that way.'

'Don't be,' she snapped. 'I'm sure Miss Mills will fully occupy your time in future.'

'No doubt,' he rasped. 'Last night hasn't—affected your relationship with Malcolm?'

'Not at all,' she answered truthfully. 'You see, like you, I realised it was a mistake, and I told him so.'

'It meant nothing to you?'

'It meant the end of a relationship that's lingered on far too long already. So don't worry about me, Joel, you're perfectly free to see whoever you want without condemnation from me.'

'As you are,' he bit out harshly.

'As I am,' she nodded. 'I'm sure Miss Mills will be wonderful for "Witchcraft".'

He nodded tersely. 'The name of the product suits her well,' he muttered as he left.

It was only once he had gone that Lindsay realised the tension she had been under, and she relaxed slowly, refusing to let the tears fall as they clouded her eyes. She had cried her last tears over Joel, she refused to let him hurt her again.

But that was so much easier said than done. Almost daily, it seemed, Marilyn Mills came to the studio, even on the days she wasn't needed to work, and invariably Joel took the other woman to lunch. It was painful torture for Lindsay to watch them together, and she felt grateful for the fact that she had finally managed to get another job, one that promised to be as interesting as working at the studio. The secretary to a top designer in one of the exclusive salons in town had decided to leave and train to be a model herself, leaving an opening. With her working background and experience Lindsay had felt quite confident when she went to the interview, liking Kay instantly. The other girl seemed to feel the same way about her, for a letter offering her the job arrived two days later. Of course she had accepted.

Pleased by her good fortune, Lindsay had informed Joel of her plans, receiving only lukewarm interest for her trouble. He was very withdrawn nowadays, no explosions of temper or sarcasm, just a cold curtness that she found she hated.

Malcolm had returned to America for a few weeks, leaving a devastated Judi behind him, although her sister still wouldn't admit that to the man himself, remaining wary of this man who had bulldozed his way into her life.

'Stubbornness,' Lindsay taunted her when she went

home for the weekend before her last week of working for Joel, she and her mother having attained an uneasy truce, a truce that lasted as long as the subject of Joel wasn't mentioned. And that suited Lindsay perfectly, she had no wish to talk about him either.

'Not at all,' Judi dismissed. 'I have every intention of agreeing to marry him when he returns.'

'You do?' she said excitedly.

Her sister nodded. 'Provided he asks me, of course,' she mocked her own forwardness.

'Oh, he will,' Lindsay assured confidently. 'He calls every night, doesn't he?'

Judi nodded. 'Much to Mother's delight.'

'Well, at least she does approve of Malcolm,' Lindsay grimaced. 'Think what it would be like if she didn't!'

'I'd marry him anyway,' Judi told her simply.

'You really do love him, don't you?' Lindsay realised delightedly. 'I'm so glad.'

Judi pulled a face. 'I don't think I had much choice, with the two of you ganging up against me! I—I told him about Jonathan when he called last night,' she revealed huskily. 'He was very understanding.'

Lindsay knew that talking to Malcolm about Jonathan was the final barrier, that the other couple were indeed going to be happy together.

Her own happiness was no longer something she even thought about, and as the next week sped by she faced the final goodbye from Joel, knowing they weren't likely to meet again, not even socially, although she had no doubt Cally would try to get them together some time in the future. The other woman was still convinced they were meant for each other, something she told Lindsay each time she telephoned for a chat. Lindsay didn't like to disillusion her, so she didn't contradict her.

The last week was the hardest of all, although her time was pretty well occupied with training her successor. Shirley Rand was a pretty young housewife, several years older than Lindsay, and her enthusiasm for the job of being Joel's secretary made up for her inexperience. And Joel was polite enough to her, which was something, knowing he could make life very unpleasant if he didn't like someone. Although Shirley was so nice it was hard for anyone not to like her.

'No little friend today?' queried a condescending voice that Lindsay instantly recognised—and as usual disliked.

Lindsay looked up with a start, not having heard the other woman come in, although she should have smelt the perfume, as she had the first day she had met this woman. Nothing had changed between the two of them, they still treated each other with veiled dislike. Marilyn Mills was so confident of herself where Joel was concerned now that she didn't always try to hide her contempt for Lindsay.

She looked at the other woman resignedly. 'If you're talking about Shirley then she's gone to lunch.'

Marilyn made herself comfortable in one of the armchairs, lighting up a cigarette. 'She seems a very nice girl, in an innocuous way,' she drawled.

'She is nice,' Lindsay nodded, deciding that even though she didn't like this woman's condescending tone about Shirley, with only one more day to go she could manage to be polite.

'And married,' Marilyn said with obvious satisfaction.

She frowned. 'Yes.'

'Happily, I gather.'

'Miss Mills——'

'Forget the polite formality when we're alone,' the other woman snapped irritably. 'It's as phoney as you are.'

Lindsay's eyes widened at this sudden attack after weeks of cool disdain. 'I'm afraid I——'

'Let's at least admit to ourselves that we can't stand each other,' Marilyn sneered.

She flushed. 'I've never pretended I felt any differently.'

'No, you haven't, have you,' the other woman realised thoughtfully. 'Had Joel already told you about me?'

'No, of course not. Joel doesn't discuss his personal life with anyone.'

'No,' Marilyn acknowledged. 'At least, not usually. But then that depends who he's talking to, doesn't it? You see, I know all about you.'

Lindsay stiffened. 'Really?'

Marilyn gave a husky laugh. 'Don't look so disapproving! Of course Joel told me about the two of you. He isn't a man who likes deceit.'

'No,' she acknowledged curtly.

'Of course I was relieved when you had resigned as his secretary rather than my having to ask Joel to get rid of you,' Marilyn continued in a bored voice. 'It prevented things from becoming really nasty.'

Lindsay was rigid with indignation. 'You seem very confident that Joel would have done as you asked.'

Marilyn gave her a malicious smile. 'Don't you think he would have done?'

Lindsay flushed her resentment. 'It was never put to the test, was it?'

'Luckily for you,' the other woman drawled dismissively.

Much as she hated to admit it, Lindsay thought Marilyn might be right. Joel seemed to see the other woman every day, and although it didn't seem to be making him happy he kept going back for more. No doubt Marilyn had more influence with him than Lindsay had ever had.

'I believe Joel is free now if you want to go in, and——'

'But I'm enjoying our little chat so much, Lindsay,' Marilyn cut in smoothly. 'We've had so little time to talk privately together, although I'm sure you can understand that Mrs Rand is so much more suitable as Joel's secretary now that I'm back in his life. It would hardly be fitting for you to continue working for him when I'm his wife.'

Lindsay controlled her shaking hands with effort, too shocked to hide her reaction completely. To think of Joel marrying this woman nauseated her. She moistened suddenly dry lips. 'When is the wedding to be?' Her voice was unnaturally brittle.

'Did I mention a wedding?' Marilyn mocked. 'I don't think you quite understand, Lindsay. I still use my professional name of Mills when I'm working, but my name actually became Sutherland seven years ago!'

CHAPTER EIGHT

LINDSAY was dumbstruck by this information, although it did seem to make Joel's aversion to marriage all the more understandable; how could he offer marriage to any woman when he was already married? Nevertheless, she still questioned the truth of his marriage to this woman; she hadn't believed Joel capable of such deceit.

'You're divorced?' she frowned.

Marilyn shook her head. 'There was never a divorce.'

Lindsay swallowed hard. 'Then you and he—You're still married to each other?'

'As I said,' the other woman shrugged uninterestedly, 'there was never a divorce.'

Lindsay found it difficult to think of Joel married to this woman, especially for the last seven years. And if they had lived apart all this time why *hadn't* they divorced?

Marilyn seemed to guess some of what she was thinking. 'Of course, like a lot of couples, we've had our problems, but as you can see, we're well and truly back together now. By the way,' she added, her eyes narrowed, 'you left an ornate comb at Joel's apartment, I must remember to post it to you some time. Maybury was quite embarrassed when I asked him if he knew who it belonged to,' she revealed dryly.

Lindsay noticed Joel hadn't felt the same emotion! 'Don't bother to send it back to me,' she dismissed abruptly. 'I have plenty of other combs.'

'But this is such a pretty one,' Marilyn persisted. 'Brown shot through with gold.'

Lindsay knew the comb instantly, although she couldn't say she had missed it. How awful that this woman should be the one to find it. 'It's quite inexpensive,' she shrugged. 'The gold isn't real.'

'What a pity,' Marilyn mocked softly. 'I'll send it to you, anyway.'

'Please don't bother,' requested Lindsay through gritted teeth, knowing she would never wear the comb again now anyway; each time she did it would remind her of Joel and this woman living together.

'It's really no bother,' Marilyn drawled. 'And in a way it helped me to know your taste in jewellery. Joel and I picked the gift out together that he's going to give you tomorrow when you leave—I hope you like it.'

Whatever it was Lindsay hated it already! 'Joel had no need to buy me anything—after all, I chose to leave.'

'I believe it's the customary thing to do,' Marilyn dismissed in a bored voice.

'Perhaps,' she acknowledged tightly, although she would still rather Joel hadn't done it, and especially wished he hadn't taken this woman with him to choose it; it wouldn't even be something she could cherish and always think of as something Joel had given her, knowing it would remind her more of his wife than of Joel.

'I'm sure you'll like it,' the other woman smiled. 'I'll go in and see Joel now.'

As far as Lindsay was concerned she could stay in with him all day if she wanted to; but she couldn't stay around and watch it. She had received a severe shock today, and as soon as Shirley returned from lunch she made her excuses and left for the day, needing desperately to be alone.

Would the pain of loving Joel never be over? How could he have kept something so important as his marriage a secret from her? Because she didn't doubt it was the truth, Marilyn wasn't stupid enough to claim something as fact that could so easily be disproved. And Joel had known how she would feel about his marriage, had realised she would never consider becoming involved with him if she had known, which was precisely the reason he hadn't told her.

But she kept to her promise to herself not to cry over him any more, even though her throat and her head ached from the effort it took her to hold the tears inside her. Damn Joel to hell, why did he have to be *married*, how could he do that to her!

It was obvious from what the other woman had said that she had moved back in with him, that they had now resumed their marriage, that Joel had even told Marilyn about their own relationship. Perhaps he had needed to tell her everything after Marilyn had found her comb!

The last thing Lindsay expected was to find Joel on her doorstep at six-thirty!

'Yes?' She kept him standing there, her behaviour definitely hostile.

'Shirley said you left early because you weren't feeling well,' he frowned his concern. 'I thought I would just come and check that you're okay now.'

Her mouth was tight. 'Wouldn't a telephone call have sufficed?' she said waspishly.

He seemed puzzled by her cold manner. His face had lost some of its healthy tan the last few weeks, and he looked thinner. His hair was longer than he usually wore it to, as if he hadn't had time lately to worry too much about his appearance, even his navy blue three-piece suit did not fit as well as it did normally.

'I wanted to see for myself that you're all right.' He spoke quietly.

Lindsay still held the door firmly closed, only opening it enough to be able to see him clearly. 'As you can see,' her voice was brittle, 'I'm perfectly all right.'

Still he made no effort to leave. 'Shirley said something about a headache . . .?'

'Yes,' she snapped.

'Do you still have it?'

'Joel——'

'You look very pale.' He was watching her closely. 'Are you sure it's just a headache?'

'Of course I'm sure,' she bit out impatiently. 'Now if you'll excuse me——'

'Lindsay, I have to talk to you.' He pushed the door with enough force to open it, taking her arm to guide her back into the lounge after closing the flat door behind them.

She wrenched away from him. 'I don't feel like talking to you! I told you, I still have a headache——'

'I'm not convinced you ever had a headache,' he told her grimly.

'I don't lie, Joel, not even about something as trivial as that.' Her voice was all the more forceful because she knew he had lied to her, and seriously, by omission if nothing else. 'Now I'm sure I must be delaying you from being somewhere else you would much rather be.'

He looked at her wordlessly for several seconds, neither denying nor agreeing with the statement. 'Lindsay,' he finally spoke, 'are you pregnant?'

Her mouth almost fell open in her surprise, and she looked up at Joel's grim face disbelievingly. 'I—What did you just say?' she choked her shock.

He gave a sigh, shrugging the broadness of his shoulders, as if he no more liked what he was saying than she did. 'I didn't mean for it to come out that bluntly——'

'Bluntly!' she echoed disbelievingly. 'That was—It was incredible! You come here uninvited, force your way in, and then come out with a question like *that*! God, I still can't believe you said it!'

Joel ran a hand through the unruly thickness of his hair, making it even more dishevelled. 'You haven't looked too well lately, and——'

'Does that give you the right to make wild accusations like that?' she scorned harshly.

'It wasn't an accusation, Lindsay,' he said wearily. 'The last time we were together I—we—I wasn't as careful as I should have been.'

'The so-cautious Joel Sutherland forgot to take precautions!' she scoffed.

'I didn't forget,' an angry flush darkened his cheeks just above the jawbone. 'I just didn't come to your apartment that night expecting—prepared, to stay.'

'Really?' Lindsay's voice was shrill with scepticism; she was all the more angry herself because it wasn't until days afterwards that she had given the idea of pregnancy a thought. Joel's worry seemed a little late in coming now. 'I had the impression *that* was exactly what you came here for!'

'Lindsay——'

'Well, you can put your mind at rest,' she told him with distaste. 'I'm not pregnant.'

'Oh.' Joel looked taken aback.

Her mouth twisted derisively. 'You might show a

little more enthusiasm for the fact that you aren't about to become a father! Unless of course Mrs Sutherland has managed to persuade you that domesticity isn't so bad.'

Joel went very still, his face suddenly haggard, his eyes a dark gold. 'What did you say?' he demanded through stiff lips, a nerve beating erratically in his jaw.

'You surely didn't think you could keep a secret like that for ever?' she taunted.

'Who told you?'

'Marilyn herself.'

'The bitch!' he ground out. 'And I'm sure she took great pleasure in doing so.'

Lindsay shrugged. 'I don't know why you had to keep it a secret anyway, it's nothing to be ashamed of.'

His eyes narrowed at this. 'Just exactly what did Marilyn tell you about us?'

'Only the barest details of the marriage.'

'Nothing else?'

'Wasn't that enough?'

He gave a heavy sigh. 'It all happened seven years ago. I've tried to forget it ever happened, and I wish she had done the same.'

'Why should she? You never did,' she mocked.

'No,' he acknowledged gruffly.

Her headache was slowly getting worse now, the dull throb becoming a painful ache. 'Now that you've satisfied your curiosity about my non-existent "condition", you might as well go.'

'I'd rather stay and talk to you.'

'What would be the point of that?' Lindsay sighed at the futility of it.

'You're leaving tomorrow,' he reminded her raggedly. 'Surely the least we can do is part as friends?'

She shook her head. 'I don't think so, Joel.'

'Lovers, then,' he ground out.

Her eyes widened in alarm at the savagery in his face. 'We stopped being that weeks ago,' she told him, although her voice lacked force.

'I don't think we'll ever stop.' His voice was compellingly low, his gaze fixed on the parted fullness of her mouth. 'I've missed you so much, Lindsay, more than I believed it possible to miss anyone.'

'That line may have worked last time, Joel,' she scorned, 'but not this time.'

'But it's the truth.'

'Did you miss having Marilyn in your bed in the same way?' she jeered bitterly.

'It isn't the same thing——'

'I agree, it isn't,' Lindsay snapped. 'The thought of you coming near me after her makes me feel ill!'

'I can't help what's happened in the past——'

'And I want no part of your future,' she told him heatedly. 'Find yourself another mistress, Joel, because I'm not interested. So if you came here tonight *prepared* to persuade me back into bed with you you're out of luck. I have one day left to work for you and then I hope never to see you again!'

'You don't mean that,' he rasped.

'Of course I mean it! Surely your conceit hasn't led you to believe I'll resume our affair once I've left your employment?' She was incredulous at the idea.

'You know about Marilyn now——'

'Not all of it,' she rasped. 'And I don't want to know either. I think the two of you are probably well matched and deserve each other!'

Joel recoiled as if she had hit him. 'Maybe we always did,' he agreed heavily. 'I'll go now—I'm sorry I bothered you.'

Lindsay regretted being so harsh with him now; she had never seen Joel so without arrogance, and she did not like it at all. 'Joel,' she put her hand towards him, 'I didn't mean——'

'God, I need to hold you one last time!' His control snapped as he took her in his arms, holding her firmly against his chest, his cheek resting against the gold of her hair.

His proximity was her undoing, the clean male smell of him, and for a moment she forgot all about his wife, the bitterness between the two of them, and pressed her cheek into his shoulder, her eyes closed as she breathed in the undeniable pleasure of being in his arms once more.

'I've needed this so badly the last few weeks,' he groaned into her hair. 'Sometimes I thought I would go insane with wanting it.'

Lindsay had wanted this too, she knew that now. 'Joel, you have to go,' she told him huskily.

'Yes.' But he made no effort to release her.

'I can't let you stay here tonight.'

'No.' Still he held her as if he never wanted to let her go.

'Please don't tempt me, Joel,' she pleaded for one of them to act sanely and remember he had a wife.

'I can't help it,' he looked down at her with golden eyes, 'I want to kiss you.'

'No!'

'Yes,' he decided firmly, his head bending as he gently claimed her mouth in a kiss that seemed to draw the very soul from her body. 'Oh, Lindsay,' he murmured shakily against her aching mouth. 'Dear God, you taste so good!'

She was a fool, she knew it even as she let him claim her mouth again, his kiss more forceful this time, parting her lips to invade her mouth with the warm hardness of his tongue. The groan of surrender seemed to come from her throat, and yet it could equally have come from Joel's, their mouths were so finely enmeshed they seemed to be one.

This time it was the ringing of the doorbell that interrupted them, pulling them apart. Joel still looked dazed from his arousal as she moved away from him, reality returning with a harshness that made her pale.

'The *second* most sadistic appliance ever invented!' Joel tried to make light of the situation, but neither of them saw any humour in it, Lindsay turning away with a sob as she moved to answer the door.

She didn't know who she was expecting her visitor to be, but certainly not Malcolm. 'I didn't think you were expected back yet,' she said dazedly as he swung her up in his arms.

'I wasn't,' he grinned down at her. 'But I—Joel,' he said slowly as he saw the other man just inside the apartment where he had followed Lindsay, turning back to her regretfully. 'I didn't realise you weren't alone.'

She put her arm through the crook of his for moral support. 'Joel was just leaving,' she said pointedly.

Malcolm raised dark brows. 'Oh?'

'Yes,' rasped Joel, his expression remote. 'I called round on a matter of—business.'

'Then don't let me interrupt you,' Malcolm said lightly. 'I'll just go into the lounge and wait for you, Lindsay.'

'Oh, but——'

'Don't be long,' he touched her cheek gently. 'I have some wonderful news to tell you. Nice to have seen you again, Joel,' he nodded to the other man.

The silence between Joel and Lindsay was almost

deafening once Malcolm had gone through to the lounge, each of them eyeing the other warily.

'I didn't know you were expecting company,' Joel finally rasped, his hands thrust into his trouser pockets, the material tight across his thighs, his arousal no longer evident.

Her mouth twisted. 'I'm sure you heard me say I wasn't expecting Malcolm back from America yet.'

'I thought that was just for my benefit,' he bit out coldly.

Lindsay flushed her anger. 'Then you thought wrong. The last I heard, Malcolm wasn't expected back for a couple of more days at least.'

Joel's gaze raked over her icily. 'It seems he couldn't keep away from you any longer!'

She had had so many occasions to tell Joel the truth about Malcolm and herself, and yet pride held her back from confiding in him, especially now, when she was once again feeling vulnerable. 'Yes,' she agreed abruptly.

'Then I won't keep *you* from him any longer,' he told her resignedly.

As he turned to leave Lindsay could almost believe he was sorry to have to go; her hand moved out as if to stop him, falling back to her side as she mentally reprimanded herself for falling for his ploy a second time in one evening. 'I'll see you tomorrow, Joel,' she said firmly.

'Lindsay, what happened before Malcolm arrived——'

'Is best forgotten,' she dismissed.

'Will you forget it?' he asked raggedly.

She swallowed hard, knowing she would never forget any of the time they had spent together. 'I already have,' she stated with cruel bluntness. 'Now I really can't keep Malcolm waiting any longer. . . .'

'No,' Joel acknowledged curtly.

Lindsay took several minutes to calm her shattered nerves before composing her features into a casually smiling mask and going in to see Malcolm. He had made himself comfortable by sprawling out in one of the armchairs, at ease in an open-necked shirt and fitted blue suit, lithely tanned and fit after his two weeks of hard work in America.

He sat forward as she came into the room, his elbows resting on his knees, a puzzled frown on his handsome face. 'You keep telling me it's over between you two, and yet it seems to me that every time I call or come here I fall over the guy, so what is going on? And don't say nothing, that's starting to wear a little thin to me.'

'Even if it's the truth?'

He gave her a chiding look. 'You don't expect me to believe that it is?'

She shrugged. 'It's your prerogative to believe what you want. Now tell me what this great news is of yours?'

'Why is it you always change the subject on me?' he grimaced.

Lindsay gave him an impish smile. 'Because your questions are always too personal.'

Malcolm somehow managed to look offended. 'I haven't kept any secrets from you.'

'Only because you needed my help to try and trap my poor sister!'

He gave a wide, satisfied grin. 'Talking of Judi . . .'

'Yes?' she prompted excitedly.

Malcolm gave a nonchalant shrug. 'Well, I've been calling her from New York every evening——'

'I know *that*!' she told him impatiently.

'But you didn't know that last night when I spoke to

her I proposed—and she accepted!' he announced triumphantly.

Lindsay blinked her astonishment—not that Judi and Malcolm were getting married, but that her sister had accepted a proposal over the telephone. It didn't sound like the reserved Judi at all.

'Don't look so surprised!' Malcolm spluttered with laughter. 'She happens to love me.'

'Oh, I know that,' she dismissed. 'But I somehow never thought of Judi becoming engaged over the telephone.'

'She hasn't.' He reached into the pocket of his jacket to take out a brown velvet ring box. 'When I put this on her finger we'll be engaged. Which is precisely the reason I'm here to see you.'

'Sorry?' she frowned, having lost him along the way somewhere.

'Judi wanted to call you and tell you the good news, but I persuaded her it would be more fun this way. Change your clothes, put on your make-up, do whatever you have to do to be ready to drive down to see Judi in ten minutes.'

Lindsay shook her head. 'I'm sure you don't want me around when you give Judi her ring.'

'I want the whole family there,' he told her confidently. 'You're all invited out to dinner.' He glanced at the plain gold watch on his wrist. 'And if you don't hurry up we'll be late. I told Judi we would be there by eight o'clock.'

'She does know about all this then?'

'Of course she knows—I just told you I proposed to her, she accepted, and——'

'I meant the dinner party,' Lindsay cut in derisively.

'Judi is organising it. Although if her rather

sceptical young sister doesn't hurry herself the party is going to be minus one—and I don't mean me,' he looked at her pointedly beneath lowered lashes.

'Okay, I'm going,' she laughed. 'I have a feeling poor Judi doesn't quite know how forceful her husband is going to be,' she couldn't resist adding mockingly.

Not that Judi looked as if she cared how forceful he was when they arrived a short time later, launching herself into Malcolm's waiting arms, oblivious of everyone else, and Lindsay wisely moved quietly into the house to give them a few minutes' privacy.

It was a happy evening for all of them, Judi glowingly happy as the emerald and diamond ring glittered on her left hand, Malcolm looking for all the world as if he had been given a far greater treasure than any jewel in the world, Mike thinking it great that his sister was marrying such a man, and even their mother seeming proud as the wedding was discussed for Christmas.

The family party continued when they got back to the house, Lindsay and Malcolm finally deciding to stay the night and drive back to town early the next morning. Which was exactly what they did, arriving back in London at seven o'clock, which gave Lindsay plenty of time to get ready for work.

The dinner party the evening before, and talking softly to Judi long after everyone else was asleep, had helped take her mind off the fact that she left the studio today. Although she was very aware of it as she prepared for her last day of working for Joel, applying her make-up carefully, her hair newly washed and gleaming, the simply cut black dress she wore giving her a look of extreme elegance.

Not that Joel seemed aware of her appearance when

he arrived shortly after she did, not even seeming to notice her presence there at all, let alone acknowledge the fact that he had been in her apartment the evening before.

Well, that suited her just fine. She wanted to keep everything between them impersonal until the very last minute she left here. Judi and Malcolm's uncomplicated happiness in each other the evening before had shown her how futile her own aspirations for Joel and herself had been.

But her desire not to be alone with him again seemed fated to be unsuccessful when he invited her out to lunch later that morning.

'I'd rather not,' she refused as gracefully as she could in front of Shirley, knowing that if they had been alone she would have flatly refused him. He probably knew it too!

'It's your last day, Lindsay,' he encouraged softly. 'Surely you wouldn't deny your boss the privilege of buying you lunch as a thank-you for all the work you've done for me the last year?'

He had put her in an awkward position in front of the other woman, and this time she was *sure* he knew it. 'When you put it like that . . .'

'I do,' he said with satisfaction.

'. . . then I'm sure Shirley and I would love to go to lunch with you,' she finished sweetly.

'Oh, but——'

'Wouldn't we, Shirley?' she interrupted the other girl's refusal.

Shirley looked disconcerted. 'I'm sure Joel would rather it were just the two of you.'

Lindsay looked at him challengingly. 'Would you?'

The look he gave her spoke volumes, although as she had already known, he couldn't say too much in front of his new secretary. 'Of course not,' he said smoothly. 'The more the merrier. Perhaps you could confirm the reservation at the Ritz,' he instructed Lindsay distantly.

'The Ritz!' Shirley repeated excitedly once Joel had returned to his studio. 'I've only ever looked inside the door before. Have you ever been there?'

On an occasion Lindsay would rather forget, along with everything else about Joel Sutherland. They had been at the Ritz the night he had asked her to move in with him, and the two of them had made it into a night of celebration once she had agreed. She had a feeling Joel had chosen that particular restaurant on purpose.

'Once,' she answered abruptly.

'Is it as fantastic as they say?' Shirley seemed not to notice her lack of enthusiasm.

'Yes,' she bit out, picking up the telephone. 'I'd better confirm the reservation.'

She was more than relieved that she had thought to include Shirley once she got through to the restaurant and was told Mr Sutherland already had a secluded table for two booked, knowing that Joel had intended it to be so much more than a thank-you lunch from a boss to his secretary, and she changed the reservation to three. And she had another reason to be grateful Shirley would be present at the luncheon, having a feeling Joel was going to give her the piece of jewellery then that he and his wife had picked out for her together!

CHAPTER NINE

SHIRLEY was suitably impressed by the inside of the Ritz, revelling in the attentive service, seeming unaware of the tension that was so tangible to Lindsay. To all intents and purposes Joel was being the perfect host to them both, attentive to their every need, but Lindsay was very much aware of his brooding glance as it remained fixed on her.

When Shirley excused herself to go to the powder-room Lindsay knew the silence between Joel and herself would finally be broken.

'Inviting Shirley along for lunch wasn't fair, Lindsay,' he told her softly.

She looked across at him with challenging green eyes. 'Not fair to whom?'

'To her, of course.' His hand moved to cover hers as it rested on the table-top, refusing to release her as she tried in vain to pull away.

She shrugged. 'She's having a wonderful time.'

He nodded. 'But sensing more and more every moment that she's an unwanted third.'

'As far as I'm concerned that's *you*!' She glared at him.

'Did you have a nice evening yesterday after I'd gone?' he rasped suddenly.

Her expression softened slightly as she thought of the previous evening. 'Very nice.'

'Where did you go?'

She looked up at him sharply. 'What makes you think we went anywhere?'

'I telephoned your flat at eleven-thirty, and there was no answer,' he revealed grimly.

'Then I obviously did go out.' Her sarcasm was obvious.

His hand tightened on hers. 'I also tried again at twelve o'clock, twelve-thirty, one o'clock——! Where the hell were you?' he demanded to know fiercely.

His hand was crushing hers until she almost cried out with the pain, but she refused to even wince. 'We went out to dinner, and by that time it was so late I didn't bother to go home.'

'Didn't bother——? Where could you have gone to have dinner that it was too late to drive home?'

'Cambridgeshire,' she told him pointedly.

His hand relaxed slightly on hers, as if realising he must be hurting her. 'You went to your mother's house,' he realised raggedly.

'After dinner,' she nodded.

Joel's mouth was taut with tension. 'I take it your family approve of Malcolm?'

'Wholeheartedly!'

He released her hand with an uneven sigh. 'Then he has it all, doesn't he—you and family approval.'

Her eyes flashed her anger. 'You could have had them too once, but making an impression on my family never interested you!'

'Surely you can understand why now?' he rasped. 'I've made too much of a mess of my life to want to drag you down into it on a permanent basis.'

'Meeting my family wouldn't have committed you to anything!' Lindsay snapped.

'Does it commit Malcolm to anything?'

She was breathing heavily in her agitation, wanting to hurt him as he continued to hurt her. 'The wedding is planned for Christmas,' she told him abruptly.

Joel's hand fell away from her completely, his face white and haggard. 'You're going to *marry* him?'

'I——'

'Even the Ladies is fantastic!' Shirley told them breathlessly as she sat down.

Joel seemed too shaken to answer her, so it was left up to Lindsay to do so. 'It is very nice here, but if we're all finished now . . .' she added pointedly, not wanting to prolong this any longer than necessary, not really sure, when it came down to it, if she could actually have lied and told Joel she was going to marry Malcolm. She hoped she hadn't been reduced to that!

'Yes, it is getting late,' giggled Shirley, having imbibed a little too much of the excellent wine.

Their host still seemed lost in thought. 'Joel?' Lindsay prompted him.

'Yes,' he said abruptly, signalling for the bill. 'Damn, I almost forgot,' he muttered as he reached into his inside pocket for his wallet, and taking out a long thin jewellery case instead. 'This is for you, Lindsay,' he told her huskily, holding out the case.

It was the moment she had been dreading, and her hand shook slightly as she took the velvet case, knowing by Shirley's excited expression that she at least was looking forward to seeing what was inside.

Nestled against the black velvet was a golden charm bracelet, containing about twenty charms. Lindsay's quick glance took in a typewriter and a camera, not wanting to see what else there was on it, knowing that the charms were too personal to their past relationship, and that Joel had chosen them with Marilyn Sutherland, his wife.

'It's lovely, thank you,' she accepted raggedly, closing the box with a firm snap.

'Aren't you going to wear it now?' Shirley looked disappointed.

She shook her head. 'I wouldn't want to lose one of the charms before I've had time to have them put on properly.'

'They're already soldered on, if that's what you're worried about,' Joel told her abruptly.

'Oh.' Guilty colour darkened her cheeks, knowing it would feel like a manacle about her wrist if she had to wear the bracelet. 'Well, it might be a little awkward to type in it,' she excused awkwardly.

Joel's expression was harsh as he guessed her reluctance to wear the gift. 'I don't expect you to work on your last afternoon.'

She couldn't imagine what else he expected her to do! Besides, the time would drag by too slowly if she just sat around doing nothing. 'I'd prefer to finish off my work before I leave,' she told him abruptly.

He looked for a moment as if he might argue with that, and then he shrugged. 'We may as well get back, then.'

'Isn't it a beautiful bracelet?' Shirley sighed her admiration once they were back at the studio.

'Very nice.' And Lindsay doubted she would ever look at it again! 'Play your cards right and you could get one just like it when you leave,' she teased lightly.

'Peter would probably wonder what I'd done to earn—— Oh!' Shirley broke off awkwardly, her face full of contrition. 'I didn't mean that the way it sounded.'

'I know you didn't,' Lindsay sympathised with the girl's embarrassment, although she was also a little shaken by it.

'I'm sure Joel only bought you the bracelet in

appreciation for all the work you've done for him.' Shirley tried to make good her slip of the tongue.

'I'm sure he did too,' Lindsay nodded. 'She had known the other girl must be wondering at her reason for leaving such a well paid and interesting job, she would wonder herself if the positions were reversed, and it didn't surprise her that Shirley's fervent imagination had come up with such an answer. Especially as it was the true one.

In the end her final parting from Joel came as something of an anti-climax after weeks of waiting for it to happen, Joel having to leave for a business appointment shortly before four, stopping briefly in front of her desk to say a terse goodbye.

As she watched him leave she had great difficulty in holding back the tears, and she left at five o'clock with another headache due to suppressed grief, saying her goodbye to Shirley with real regret. As soon as she reached her flat she opened the bottom drawer of her dressing-table, moving the sweaters aside to push the jewellery case to the back of the drawer, never wanting to see the bracelet again.

Kay Adams was like a whirlwind to work for. The salon was extremely busy, even more so than usual with the new autumn collection to prepare for.

Lindsay loved the place and the people from the first day she walked in, and now, after five weeks, she couldn't imagine working anywhere else. She didn't even have time to think of Joel, so engrossed was she in the work, often staying late into the evenings to help Kay, her duties including so much more than secretarial ones.

If that meant her social life was down to nil she didn't particularly care, having no interest in seeing anyone for the moment anyway. And if she didn't have the time so much the better.

After months of hard work the day to show the Collection finally arrived, and helping out behind the scenes Lindsay was caught up in the excitement of it all.

'Go and sit out front for the second half of the show,' Kay encouraged her, a slightly plump blonde who nevertheless always managed to look elegant, 'and let me know the audience reaction.'

'They love it and you know it,' Lindsay laughed, feeling as elated as everyone else involved in presenting the Collection, was sure it was already a success.

'I'd still like to know what's being said.' Kay pushed her towards the side door. 'Go on, I've had a seat kept for you near the front.'

Lindsay sat down among the glittering audience, recognising several titled ladies, a few actresses, and several other elegantly attired women who definitely acted as if they were 'someone' even if they weren't.

'Fantastic, isn't it?' said an excited voice behind her. She turned sharply. 'Cally!' she recognised with pleasure. 'I haven't seen you in weeks.'

'It's months, actually,' Cally rebuked dryly. 'I know you've been avoiding me.'

Lindsay blushed her guilt, having refused several dinner invitations from the other woman in the last few weeks. 'I've been very busy,' she excused herself.

Cally nodded. 'Joel told me you were working here,' she smiled. 'Do you like it?'

'Can't you tell?' grinned Lindsay, refusing to let even a mention of Joel ruin this day for her.

'Kay is very talented, isn't she?' Cally acknowledged.

'And nice with it.'

'Nicer to work for than Joel?' the other woman asked lightly.

This time a shadow did pass over Lindsay's face, although it was quickly erased. 'Infinitely,' she replied with feeling. 'Now tell me what you really think of the Collection,' she changed the subject.

That it was a success she never doubted, the enthusiastic comments of those around her quickly confirming it, so much so that within a few minutes she made her excuses to Cally and returned to tell Kay of her triumph.

But the work was still far from over, seemingly hundreds of newspapers wanting to take photographs of the models in different outfits before they could even begin the long process of clearing up.

'And not one of them will do justice to all my hard work,' muttered Kay as the photographers crowded the changing rooms. 'Insensitive clods!'

'They're all professionals,' Lindsay replied absently, intent on finding all the accessories that had been thrown off with more haste than care as each model hurried to change into her next outfit.

'I need a specialist, not a professional.' Kay watched the photographers worriedly. 'Thank God I have Joel to do the magazine photographs for me. Now there's a man who can appreciate style.'

Lindsay gave up looking for the left shoe to go with the right one she held in her hand. 'Joel?' she repeated woodenly.

'Your ex-employer, love,' Kay answered vaguely. 'I'll just go and rescue my models, and then I have to meet with some buyers for a late dinner.'

'But——'

'I'm afraid it's all far from over,' Kay sighed, not

noticing Lindsay's distraction. 'I'll be up most of the night talking to buyers, and we still have another show for tomorrow to do.' She rushed off, dispersing the photographers, while Lindsay and the other assistants went through the inventory late into the evening to make sure everything was prepared for the next day.

It wasn't until Lindsay fell exhausted into bed shortly after midnight that she gave any more thought to what Kay had said about Joel. Not that she needed to worry too much about seeing Joel again herself; although she had helped out with the show she was actually only Kay's secretary and need have no contact with the official photographers of the Collection.

The next day was just as hectic as the previous one had been, and Lindsay could only wonder where Kay got her energy from when she had been up talking to buyers until the early hours of the morning.

'Necessity,' she smiled when Lindsay mentioned it to her. 'If no one buys I go out of business. I—Oh no!' she groaned, looking past Lindsay. 'She's all I need right now!'

Lindsay turned to view the cause of her employer's displeasure, recognising Marilyn Sutherland instantly. The other woman looked as beautiful as ever; the autumn weather was not really cold enough for the silver-coloured fur coat she wore, although there could be no doubting the effect it made against her dark hair.

'Kay!' she purred recognition of the older woman. 'And Lindsay,' she looked at her with glittering green eyes. 'You're looking well,' she said as if she hadn't expected it to be so.

'So are you,' Lindsay returned politely.

Marilyn turned back to Kay. 'Marvellous Collection, darling,' she drawled condescendingly.

'I thought so,' Kay wasn't impressed by the sugary insincerity. 'Now if you'll excuse us . . .'

'I realise you're busy,' Marilyn nodded haughtily, 'but I had to take this opportunity to say hello to Lindsay—Joel would never forgive me if I didn't.'

Lindsay blanched at the other woman's casual claim to knowing Joel's emotions, at the same time letting Lindsay know that the reconciliation was still very much back on.

'Well, you've said it now,' Kay cut in brusquely as Lindsay seemed speechless. 'And we still have a lot to do, I'm sure you understand?'

'Of course.' Marilyn's voice was still friendly, but her eyes flashed her resentment at this dismissal. 'Nice to have seen you again, Lindsay. I'll tell Joel how much you're enjoying your new job.'

'She reminds me of a black widow spider,' muttered Kay with distaste as Marilyn left them in a cloud of her perfume. 'She entices a man into her web, uses him until there's nothing left, and then casts him aside.'

Lindsay felt some of her tension leave her now that Marilyn had left. 'I take it you don't like the lovely Miss Mills?'

Kay grimaced. 'I can't stand the woman. She worked for me for a while years ago; she thought she could tell *me* what to do!'

Lindsay grinned at her employer's disgust, knowing that no matter how friendly and easygoing Kay appeared to be on the surface she had to be made of steel underneath, dealing in the strenuous and often secret profession that she did.

But that brief encounter with Marilyn had disturbed Lindsay somewhat, and she was glad of the hectic pace of the day to stop her dwelling on it.

The next day proved to be as busy, with buyers calling at the salon all day. Kay was constantly with one group of people or another, and Lindsay was unprepared for the sight of Joel striding into the predominantly female domain mid-morning, knowing all the colour must have left her face as he came over to her desk.

'Lindsay,' he greeted her gruffly, his eyes dark as he looked down at her.

Whether or not he was happy now that he was back with his wife, the last five weeks hadn't been kind to him. His face had lost its healthy tan and was very gaunt, his tailored suit quite loose on him. His hair had been cut now, but that just seemed to accentuate how hollow his cheeks had become. What was it Kay had said about Marilyn—once she had caught her man she used him until there was nothing left and then cast him aside? Joel looked as if he were dangerously close to that now!

'Joel,' Lindsay greeted him coolly, knowing of no polite comment she could make without sounding insincere. He didn't look well, so she couldn't say that, and it certainly wasn't nice to see him, so she couldn't say that either!

He seemed to feel the same way about talking to her. 'How do you like working for Kay?' he asked.

'I love it,' she answered truthfully.

He nodded, as if it was what he had expected. 'You've been busy?'

'Very,' she said abruptly, wondering how much longer she could continue this stilted conversation.

'How are the wedding plans coming along?'

She stiffened. 'Very well,' she told him curtly.

He gave a heavy sigh. 'Don't forget to send me an invitation.'

'I——'

'Just so that I can refuse, of course,' he continued with hard derision.

'Of course,' she echoed with sweet sarcasm. 'I'll find Kay and tell her you're here.'

He held up his hand to stop her standing up. 'Don't bother, I can find her myself.'

'Oh, but——'

'Don't look so serious, Lindsay,' he mocked her earnest expression. 'I probably know this salon better than you do.'

That certainly seemed to be the case, when he managed to locate Kay within minutes, and the two of them were immersed in photographing the collection for the rest of the day. Lindsay was called in to help during the afternoon, but fortunately her contact with Joel was kept to a minimum.

Kay came into the office at eight-thirty, yawning tiredly, her eyes widening as she saw Lindsay was still there. 'I thought you went home hours ago,' she frowned.

Despite feeling as tired as Kay looked, Lindsay hadn't wanted to go home tonight; she knew that this time, after seeing Joel himself, she wouldn't be able to put the thought of him from her mind, no matter how exhausted she was. 'I'm just finishing up,' she smiled.

Kay lay full length on the burgundy-coloured leather sofa that took up the most of one wall. 'I didn't expect this sort of dedication to duty,' she murmured.

Lindsay frowned. 'Sorry?'

Kay gave her a weak smile. 'Before you came to work for me I was a bit sceptical that I was doing the right thing by employing you. Your references looked good, but as one of them was written by Joel . . .'

Lindsay was suddenly rigid with tension. 'Yes?'

'I know he can be a cold-blooded devil at times, but he can also do things that seem completely out of character. When I told him my secretary was leaving and he mentioned your name . . .!' She shrugged. 'I was more than a little wary, I can tell you. But he's always been a good friend, so I agreed to see you. I'm happy to say you're as dedicated and efficient a secretary as he told me you were.'

Lindsay swallowed hard. 'But you didn't think I would be?'

Kay shrugged. 'Joel is notorious for discarding his women as soon as they no longer interest him, and that could be a little more difficult to do if the woman is your secretary. But as soon as I met you I knew it hadn't happened that way, which only left the fact that you couldn't be all that good at your job.' She frowned suddenly. 'You're the best secretary I've ever had. I still haven't worked out why Joel would want to lose you.'

'He didn't, it was my decision to leave,' Lindsay revealed through stiff lips.

'Ah,' Kay nodded understanding. 'Making it awkward for you, was he? You must be a first, not many women would turn down the interest of a man like Joel.'

'No,' Lindsay acknowledged dully. 'I—Would you mind if I left now?'

'Go ahead,' the other woman invited tiredly. 'I'll be leaving myself as soon as I have enough energy to get up off this sofa.'

Lindsay was almost halfway home before anger engulfed her, and instead of going back to her flat as she had planned to do she went towards the other side of town, to Joel's apartment. How dared he interfere in her life in that way, especially when he knew how she had felt about Paul Robards' attitude towards her at their interview? By interfering in the way that he had he had given the wrong impression about them. Worst of all, it seemed he was responsible for her actually getting the job with Kay, thus making her indebted to him.

She didn't even care if she had to confront him and Marilyn; they were all aware of the relationship they had once shared.

Maybury opened the door to her, a tall imposing man in his late fifties. He had somewhat overawed Lindsay when she first moved in with Joel, but she had soon learnt that his autocratic features and sometimes distant manner concealed a warmth that had soon included her.

'Miss Lindsay,' he greeted in a pleased voice. 'How lovely to see you!'

'And you, Maybury.' She gave him a bright smile. 'Is Mr Sutherland at home?'

'Yes. But——'

'Mrs Sutherland?'

He frowned. 'No. But——'

'Then could you tell Joel I'm here?' She smiled to take the sting out of her tone. She had no quarrel with this man, often wondering why he put up with Joel's terseness, although there seemed to be a genuine affection between the two men.

'I'll tell him,' he nodded. 'But he could be a few minutes, he's in the bath.'

'In that case I'll tell him myself,' she said lightly.

Maybury looked slightly overwhelmed by this turn of events, not quite sure what was going on. 'Very well,' he said dazedly. 'You know the way.'

'Oh yes.' Her smile was taut as she went into Joel's bedroom, the bedroom she had once shared with him, and into the adjoining bathroom.

Joel lay sprawled out in the sunken circular bath that could also be used as a jacuzzi, his eyes widening in shocked surprise as she came to stand on the bath's edge.

The male perfection of his body could clearly be seen beneath the unscented water, a fact neither of them was concerned with at the moment. Although Lindsay did wonder what the glass of whisky was doing beside him on the bath's edge; she had never known him to drink in the bath before.

'This is a pleasant surprise——'

'Is it?' she interrupted his polite greeting. 'You may not think so by the time I leave!'

His frown deepened. 'Is there something wrong?'

'Wrong?' she echoed shrilly. 'Of course there's something wrong, you don't think I would be here otherwise, do you?' she scorned.

'You've found out you are pregnant after all——'

'I—am—not—pregnant!' she snapped. 'Will you just get off that subject and listen to me? What I am is angry, blazingly, *furiously*, angry.'

'I can see that——'

'You just don't understand why,' she derided heatedly. 'Then let me enlighten you. Kay has just informed me that the job I thought I got quite legitimately through an agency was really given to me because her good friend Joel asked her to do so!' She was breathing heavily at the end of her tirade.

'That isn't——'

'What I don't understand is how you managed to arrange it with the agency,' she demanded to know.

Joel shrugged. 'I knew which one you were using and telephoned them with the interview.'

'I might have guessed!' she said with disgust. 'I thought you would know how I feel about getting a job that way after the Paul Robards incident.'

'Kay is very pleased with your work——'

'That isn't the point, and you know it,' Lindsay sighed her exasperation. 'She as much as admitted that she wouldn't even have considered me if you hadn't made such a point of recommending me. Why did you do it, Joel?'

'You didn't seem to be having much luck finding another job, and that type of work is far from easy to come by.'

'Not when you have an influential ex-lover, it isn't,' she scorned.

A dark flush coloured his cheeks. 'I forced you into a situation where you had to leave your job with me, and I wanted to do something to make up for it. Was that such a bad thing to do?'

'Yes!'

'God, Lindsay, it was all I *could* do! After all,' he rasped, 'you'd managed to replace me as your lover all on your own.'

'Why, you——!' She bent down and picked up the full whisky glass, pouring the alcohol over his head, watching with satisfaction as it went over his head and face to drip down on to his shoulders.

CHAPTER TEN

SHE was as unprepared for what happened next as Joel had been for the iced whisky to be poured over him. A hand closed about her ankle as she was pulled off balance, crying out her dismay as she felt herself falling into the water below.

She landed with a resounding crash, water splashing out everywhere. She came to the surface to find her face dangerously close to Joel's as he helped steady her.

'Have you cooled off now?' he grated.

Lindsay was breathing hard in her agitation, her wet dress hampering her movement somewhat as she raised a hand to smack him across the face.

'I can see you haven't!' He arrested her hand in mid-air, twisting her arm behind her back. 'Would you prefer me to calm you down in some other way?' he threatened tautly.

Her face paled as she guessed the method he would employ, relaxing with effort. 'I'd like to get out of here now,' she said stiffly, refusing to look at him.

'By all means.' He released her. 'I don't think a cooling bath is the place for the conversation we need to have.' He stood up to help her out of the bath, uncaring of his nakedness. 'I'll just step under the shower and wash the whisky from my hair,' he added tautly. 'I would suggest you use that time to get out of those wet clothes and into my robe. I'll see you in the lounge in a few minutes.'

She would have liked to have argued with him

further, but unfortunately what he said made sense. Anyway, it was worth it just to see Maybury's face when she handed him her wet clothes to dry a few minutes later. 'I slipped,' she muttered.

His expression became deadpan, although the knowing twinkle in his eyes seemed to say he knew exactly what had occurred in the bathroom a few minutes ago.

Lindsay had worn Joel's robe often in the past—he certainly hadn't made much use of it—and as usual it swamped her, turning the sleeves back so that she could see her hands when Joel came into the lounge a few minutes later, fully dressed now, the pale lemon shirt and black trousers as loose on him as his suit had been earlier today.

'You're losing too much weight,' she said before she could stop herself, blushing as he looked at her with raised brows. 'You must be working too hard,' she mumbled.

'No harder than usual,' he drawled, moving to the drinks tray. 'Would you like something?'

'No, thanks.' She watched with concern as he poured himself another glass of whisky. 'You're drinking too much too,' she told him challengingly.

'Yes,' he acknowledged harshly, throwing the contents of the glass to the back of his throat and swallowing.

'Joel——'

'Don't, Lindsay,' he instructed roughly. 'Your concern is something I can't take. Tell me,' his voice lightened conversationally, 'are *you* happy?'

'I was—until today,' she nodded.

'And finding out I helped get your job with Kay ruined all that?' he scorned.

'I don't like being in debt to you for anything, not

even my job,' she snapped.

His mouth twisted. 'Why let it worry you? I doubt you'll work for anyone once you're Malcolm's wife.'

'I——' She clamped her lips firmly together as she realised what reply she had been about to make. 'We aren't married yet,' she bit out.

Joel frowned. 'Does that mean that there's some doubt about it?'

'It means exactly what I said,' she told him in a flustered voice. 'We aren't married yet, so my job is still important to me.'

'You didn't answer my question properly earlier,' he said slowly. 'Are you happy?'

'Are you?'

Joel looked down at the glass he had refilled with whisky. 'It must be obvious that I'm not.'

'Isn't being with Marilyn what you expected it would be?' she asked bitterly.

'Marilyn?' he frowned.

'You haven't forgotten her?' Lindsay scorned.

His expression was harsh. 'I told you once before, I can never forget her. But she's never made me happy.'

'Then why take her back?'

'Lindsay——'

Maybury's discreet cough cut in on their conversation. 'Mrs Sutherland is outside, sir,' he told Joel at his questioning look. 'I told her you were indisposed, but she insists on seeing you.'

Joel's frown turned to one of irritation. 'Delay her a couple of minutes and then show her in,' he finally said thoughtfully, turning back to Lindsay once they were alone again. 'What do you mean, "take her back"?' he prompted slowly.

She flushed. 'She told me the two of you were

reconciled. Not that I needed to be told,' she added with revulsion. 'It was already obvious.'

'I don't know what Marilyn has been telling you——'

'Of course you do!' she flared. 'I told you weeks ago.'

'You said she'd told you about her and David.'

'David?' Lindsay frowned. 'But who——'

'Joel, I refuse to be kept waiting outside like one of your women—Ah, now I see the reason for Maybury's delaying tactics.' Marilyn's sharp gaze narrowed on Lindsay wearing only Joel's robe. The scene looked damning, and Marilyn obviously thought so too, her mouth twisting derisively. 'I never thought you would have the nerve to come back here after what I told you!'

'I'd be interested to hear exactly what you did tell Lindsay.' Joel's voice was dangerously soft.

Black brows rose. 'You mean she hasn't told you herself?'

'She was just about to when you arrived,' he rasped grimly.

'How forbearing of you, Lindsay,' the other woman scorned. 'If I'd been in the same position I would have been round here screaming for the truth weeks ago.'

'Lindsay is nothing like you,' Joel bit out tautly. 'Thank God!'

Marilyn gave him a pitying glance. 'You really prefer this simpering idiot to a real woman?'

Lindsay blanched. She had felt confused by the conversation until that moment, but 'simpering idiot' or not, she knew when she was being insulted. 'I'm sure Joel can testify to the fact that I am a "real woman",' she snapped defensively.

For a moment a warm light blazed in Joel's eyes,

and then he was once again under control. 'What did you tell Lindsay about the past, Marilyn?' he persisted. 'Didn't you tell her about David?'

'David?' echoed Lindsay, once again puzzled by the mention of the other man. Who could he be? Had he been the reason they separated seven years ago?

'My brother,' Joel supplied abruptly.

'And my husband,' Marilyn drawled.

Lindsay's eyes widened. 'You were married to Joel's *brother*?' she gasped. 'But you said——'

'Yes?' Joel rasped as she broke off in confusion.

She looked towards the other woman with accusing eyes. 'Why did you lie to me?'

'Why did you believe me?' Marilyn taunted. 'Anyway, I don't believe I did lie,' she shrugged. 'My name did become Sutherland seven years ago, and David and I were certainly never divorced.'

'There wasn't time for that,' Joel said harshly.

Hard green eyes snapped with anger. 'I didn't force those pills down his throat!'

'We both forced him into a situation where he had no other choice!'

'Everyone has a choice,' Marilyn scorned. 'He just wasn't enough of a man to fight for what he wanted.'

'You?' Joel bit out with contempt.

'Yes!'

'Why should he want to fight for you when you'd just told him you were expecting another man's child!'

Lindsay watched in numbed fascination as Joel and Marilyn glared across the room at each other like the adversaries they obviously were, hate glittering in both their gazes. She knew now that Joel had never been Marilyn's husband, and yet there was still something that bound them together in their hatred.

'*Your* baby,' Marilyn told him softly, turning to

Lindsay with scornful eyes as she gasped. 'Shocked your puritan little soul at last, have I?' she sneered. 'Well, you needn't worry, it wasn't true.'

'What did you say?' Joel breathed harshly.

The black-haired women looked at him with challenging eyes. 'It wasn't your baby.'

'But——'

'I was only six weeks pregnant, Joel, not the nine I claimed to be.'

Joel was almost grey with shock, sitting down abruptly in one of the armchairs. 'You lied?' he choked.

'Yes.' Marilyn's mouth twisted.

'Why?' he groaned, his eyes pained.

'Because I was sick to death of listening to David feeling inferior to you!' she shouted at him. 'He always felt as if he was in your shadow, his talented older brother, while he had nothing. I married *him*, didn't I?'

'After seducing me almost on the eve of your wedding!'

'You didn't need much seducing!'

'No,' he admitted gruffly. 'But then you didn't tell me you were going to marry my brother.'

Marilyn gave a humourless laugh. 'That's because he hadn't asked me then.'

Joel gave her a look that clearly spoke of his disgust. 'Why did you tell David the baby was mine? You must have known what he would do.'

'I thought it would bring him to his senses, make him see that you were no better than he was. Instead he blamed himself,' she remembered angrily. 'Said he couldn't have made me happy enough. You saw the letter he left, you *know* what he said!' Her hands were clenched together in front of her.

Joel stood up as if in a daze. 'All these years you've let me go on believing I was responsible for David's death, you've let my parents go on believing it too.'

'Why should you be happy when I lost the only man I ever loved!' Marilyn spat the words at him. 'Oh yes, I loved David,' she stated at his stunned look. 'I loved him more than I ever thought possible. To himself he might have been a pale shadow of you, but to me he was everything. But he couldn't forget you had had me first, he was even suspicious when I told him about the baby. I had wanted him to be happy about it,' her voice broke emotionally, her face ravaged by grief. 'Instead he questioned our baby's parentage.' Her eyes were wild as she glared at Joel. 'I just told him what he wanted to hear. But I didn't expect him to kill himself! I would have told him the truth once I'd calmed down, he just didn't give me the chance.'

All the anger seemed to have gone out of Joel at this impassioned confession, and Lindsay's heart went out to the couple as he tried to take Marilyn in his arms to comfort her and was instantly rebuffed.

'Don't pity me, damn you!' she told him heatedly. 'Especially when I've been doing my best to ruin what you have with your little girl-friend here,' she added scornfully. 'Although it seems I've failed even to do that.'

'Marilyn, I——'

'What do you mean, you've been trying to ruin things between Lindsay and me?' Joel cut forcefully over Lindsay's sympathy. 'What did you do?'

Green eyes flashed at him. 'Whatever I did I didn't do it alone. You'd already given Lindsay the impression there was something between the two of us before I even came back to England, I just helped that idea along the way.'

'How?'

'By acting as if we were seeing each other again,' she shrugged. 'It worked perfectly. But the best part was when I told her *we* were the ones who got married seven years ago.'

Joel looked at Lindsay with pained eyes. '*That* was what she told you that day you had to leave early with a headache?'

Lindsay moistened dry lips, knowing she had misjudged him. 'Yes.'

'God!' he groaned. 'Why did you do it, Marilyn? What did you hope to achieve?'

'Your continued unhappiness!' she spat at him.

He sighed. 'You don't think I've had enough of that the last seven years, blaming myself for my brother's death, believing I wasn't worthy of finding happiness myself with the woman I loved?'

Lindsay's eyes widened at that. Could it be, dared she hope, that that was the reason Joel had rebuffed any idea of love between them?

'Don't you think I've suffered in the same way?' Marilyn snapped. 'At least you can console yourself with the fact that I failed to break the two of you up, that you're together again now.' She pulled her fur coat more securely up about her. 'I'm sure you'll be happy together, Lindsay has all the right ingredients to take a man in to happily-ever-after. Now I must go——'

'Marilyn——'

'Stay away from me, Joel,' she ordered through gritted teeth as he reached out for her. 'Maybe in twenty years or so we'll be able to at least talk to each other like civilised human beings. But until then I think it would be better if we didn't meet.'

She left a stunned silence behind her once she had

swept from the room, Joel seeming too shaken to talk, Lindsay simply not knowing what to say. The terrible tragedy that had ended one life and ruined so many others was so much worse than she had even imagined.

'Brandy?' Joel suddenly offered raggedly.

'Would you rather I left you to be alone?'

'God, no,' he said shakily, pouring two glasses of brandy and handing her one. 'Did you understand all of that?' he asked after he had taken a healthy swallow.

'Some of it,' she sipped at her own brandy.

'Then it's only fair that you should know the rest,' he told her raggedly.

'You don't have to tell me anything,' she shook her head.

He looked at her with dark eyes. 'You heard me tell Marilyn that I've always shunned the thought of finding a woman I could love because I didn't feel I had the right to that happiness when I'd seemingly ruined my brother's?' he asked gruffly. 'Well, I fell in love with you against all my own rules, and even though it's too late——'

'Too late?' she echoed sharply.

'You're going to marry Malcolm.'

Lindsay chewed on the softness of her inner lip. 'Judi is going to marry Malcolm,' she told him quietly.

Joel became suddenly still. 'Your sister is?'

She nodded. 'It was more or less love at first sight for both of them, and I think of Malcolm as a brother already.'

'Then why did you——' he broke off, sighing heavily. 'I gave you little choice, did I, with my jealous accusations.'

'Jealous, Joel?' she prompted softly.

'Lindsay, I love you. How do you really feel about me?' Some of his normal arrogance was back.

'The same way I always have.' She met his gaze steadily.

He looked disappointed. 'Oh.'

She gave a wan smile. 'Joel, when a woman, especially one as inexperienced as I was, decides to live with a man you can usually make a sure bet on the fact that she's already in love with him.'

His eyes glowed deeply golden. 'And do you—I mean, did you?'

'Yes. And yes,' she told him gently.

He swallowed convulsively. 'I won't ask you to marry me just yet——'

'Ask me, Joel,' she encouraged softly.

'Not until I've told you everything there is to know about the triangle of my brother, Marilyn and myself.'

'My answer will still be the same.'

'It might not,' he bit out harshly. 'Marilyn might have exonerated me from some of the blame for what happened, but I certainly don't come out of it untarnished.'

Lindsay moved forward to rest her head on his chest, her arms about his waist. 'I love you, Joel.' It felt so good to at last be able to say the words! 'I don't care what you've done.'

His arms tightened about her convulsively. 'I'm sorry for what I've put you through the last few months, but if it helps at all I've suffered as much as you have. When I came back from the States to find you'd walked out on me I felt as if someone had punched me between the eyes. But even then I wouldn't admit to myself how much I loved you. It wasn't until I realised how friendly you'd become with Malcolm that I had to admit to feeling jealous. I even started spying on you, driving past your flat just to see if he was there. And worst of all, I couldn't stay away from you, going to your home and forcing myself on you.'

'I don't remember any force being used,' she mumbled into his chest.

'Seductive force,' he amended defensively.

Lindsay leant back in his arms to shake her head. 'If I hadn't wanted you I wouldn't have let you stay.'

'But the next morning you evaded even talking about it.'

'I didn't want to hear you say it had been a mistake,' she corrected. 'And when Marilyn turned up that morning all sorts of thoughts went through my mind,' she admitted guiltily. 'You looked as if you'd seen a vision——'

'A ghost,' he sighed. 'A ghost I finally knew I had to face if I was to take the life I wanted with you. I didn't really leave anything in the studio that day when I went to lunch, I came back to talk to you, to try and explain about the past. Finding Malcolm there, knowing he was the one to call you the night before, I realised that I was already too late.'

Lindsay shook her head. 'You could never be that. But tell me about your brother now,' she prompted as his eyes still looked shadowed.

He gave a ragged sigh and released her, as if he couldn't be close to even her when he told her about something that was so painful to him. 'David was younger than me, by five years, and all through our childhood I knew he looked upon me as his fantastic older brother. Sometimes I must have disappointed his expectations of me, but I never did it intentionally. I loved him too, you see—I felt as much admiration for him as he did for me. When I began to do well with my camera he became my assistant. After—after he died I preferred to work alone when I could.'

She had often wondered about this preference he had, knowing things could have been a lot easier for him if he had taken on a full-time assistant. But she didn't interrupt him now, knowing he had to tell her about the past in his own way.

'Then a young green-eyed witch sent me her portfolio one day,' he recalled grimly. 'I was fascinated by the photographs, even more so by the girl herself. She seemed to feel the same way about me, and we— we became lovers. What I hadn't realised, and I doubt Marilyn had at that time either, was that David had fallen in love with her. But he said nothing, not even when the affair ended.'

'Why did it end?' Lindsay prompted.

Joel shrugged. 'I suppose because we had nothing more than physical attraction going for us. What I didn't know was that she had started seeing David shortly after that. I certainly had no idea they were getting married,' he rasped. 'The first I knew of that was when they got back from the register office. I suppose I said all the right things, but David was never convinced I truly wished them happiness.' He put up a hand over his eyes. 'You see, Marilyn had spent the night with me about a week before the wedding, and I was stunned that they were now married. David changed after that, he became morose, moody—I know now it was because he was jealous of the affair I had once had with Marilyn. I thought at the time that he'd got over that, that we were back to being brothers again. And then Marilyn told him she was pregnant. You heard why she lied to him about that,' his eyes were dark with emotion. 'We all believed her when she said she was nine weeks pregnant, and when David asked me if the child could be mine . . .' He swallowed hard. 'I thought it could, you see, and I couldn't lie to him. He went home and took a bottle of pills.'

'And his letter?'

'He said he was only in the way, that he wanted Marilyn and me to be happy together,' Joel told her gruffly. 'Marilyn instantly lost the baby, and my parents disowned me.'

'Oh no!'

'Yes,' he sighed. 'And I couldn't blame them for that. I'd as good as killed their younger son.'

'Oh, Joel!' Lindsay moved back into his arms. 'It wasn't your fault, can't you see that?'

'Not completely,' he agreed softly. 'But if I hadn't become involved with Marilyn in the first place maybe none of this would have happened.'

'It couldn't have stopped your brother feeling the way he did,' she assured him gently. 'And if he had the tendency to take his own life inside him something else would eventually have triggered it off one day.'

'Maybe you're right,' Joel nodded. 'But it doesn't make it any easier to live with. My parents have never forgiven me.'

'Have you given them the opportunity to?'

'Hm?' He looked puzzled.

'It usually takes the co-operation of both sides to heal a rift like this,' she explained softly. 'And with the chip on the shoulder you've been walking around with they wouldn't have found it easy to make the first move either! I'm not saying that's the way it is,' she touched his face with gentle fingertips. 'I'm just saying it could be.'

'Maybe,' he agreed slowly. 'Perhaps introducing them to their future daughter-in-law might break the ice?' he queried pointedly. 'Yes?' He raised dark brows.

'Yes.' She gave him a glowing smile. 'I told you my answer would still be the same.'

'So you did.' He gave a relieved smile. 'And tomorrow I'd better start convincing my future in-laws I'm worthy of becoming a member of the family.'

'And what about your future bride?' she teased.

'I'm going to start convincing her now,' he promised huskily, lifting her up in his arms.

That was what she had hoped for!

An epic novel of exotic rituals
and the lure of the Upper Amazon

THE TAKERS
RIVER OF GOLD

JERRY AND S.A. AHERN

THE TAKERS are the intrepid Josh Culhane and the seductive Mary Mulrooney. These two adventurers launch an incredible journey into the Brazilian rain forest. Far upriver, the jungle yields its deepest secret—the lost city of the Amazon warrior women!

THE TAKERS series is making publishing history. Awarded *The Romantic Times* first prize for High Adventure in 1984, the opening book in the series was hailed by *The Romantic Times* as "the next trend in romance writing and reading. Highly recommended!"

Jerry and S.A. Ahern have never been better!

A Harlequin
Signature Edition... LOVE'S
CHOICES

Penny Jordan

AUTHOR OF MORE THAN
TWENTY BEST-SELLING ROMANCES

...A TURBULENT MIX OF WORLDLY
SOPHISTICATION AND HOT-BLOODED PASSION

Available at your favorite bookstore in July, or send your name, address and zip or
postal code, along with a check or money order for $3.70 (includes 75¢ for
postage & handling) payable to Harlequin Reader Service to:

HARLEQUIN READER SERVICE:

In the U.S.	In Canada
Box 52040	5170 Yonge Street, P.O. Box 2800
Phoenix, AZ	Postal Station A
85072-2040	Willowdale, Ont. M2N 6J3

RJ-1

WORLDWIDE LIBRARY IS YOUR TICKET TO ROMANCE, ADVENTURE AND EXCITEMENT

Experience it all in these big, bold Bestsellers—Yours exclusively from WORLDWIDE LIBRARY WHILE QUANTITIES LAST

To receive these Bestsellers, complete the order form, detach and send together with your check or money order (include 75¢ postage and handling), payable to WORLDWIDE LIBRARY, to:

In the U.S.
WORLDWIDE LIBRARY
Box 52040
Phoenix, AZ
85072-2040

In Canada
WORLDWIDE LIBRARY
P.O. Box 2800, 5170 Yonge Street
Postal Station A, Willowdale, Ontario
M2N 6J3

Quant.	Title	Price
_____	**ANTIGUA KISS**, Anne Weale	$2.95
_____	**WILD CONCERTO**, Anne Mather	$2.95
_____	**STORMSPELL**, Anne Mather	$2.95
_____	**A VIOLATION**, Charlotte Lamb	$3.50
_____	**LEGACY OF PASSION**, Catherine Kay	$3.50
_____	**SECRETS**, Sheila Holland	$3.50
_____	**SWEET MEMORIES**, LaVyrle Spencer	$3.50
_____	**FLORA**, Anne Weale	$3.50
_____	**SUMMER'S AWAKENING**, Anne Weale	$3.50
_____	**FINGER PRINTS**, Barbara Delinsky	$3.50
	DREAMWEAVER,	
	Felicia Gallant/Rebecca Flanders	$3.50
_____	**EYE OF THE STORM**, Maura Seger	$3.50
_____	**HIDDEN IN THE FLAME**, Anne Mather	$3.50
	YOUR ORDER TOTAL	$_____
	New York and Arizona residents add appropriate sales tax	$_____
	Postage and Handling	$ .75
	I enclose	$_____

NAME _____

ADDRESS _____ APT.# _____

CITY _____

STATE/PROV. _____ ZIP/POSTAL CODE _____
WW2

Harlequin

Tender, captivating stories that sweep to faraway places and delight with the magic of love.

Exciting romance novels for the woman of today—a rare blend of passion and dramatic realism.

Sensual and romantic stories about choices, dilemmas, resolutions, and above all, the fulfillment of love.

GEN-A-2

Harlequin is romance...

Enter a uniquely exciting new world with

Harlequin American Romance™

Harlequin American Romances are the first romances to explore today's love relationships. These compelling novels reach into the hearts and minds of women across America... probing the most intimate moments of romance, love and desire.

You'll follow romantic heroines and irresistible men as they boldly face confusing choices. Career first, love later? Love without marriage? Long-distance relationships? All the experiences that make love real are captured in the tender, loving pages of **Harlequin American Romances**.

What makes American women so different when it comes to love? Find out with **Harlequin American Romance!**

Send for your introductory FREE book now!

Get this book FREE!

Mail to:

Harlequin Reader Service

In the U.S.
2504 West Southern Ave.
Tempe, AZ 85282

In Canada
P.O. Box 2800, Postal Station A
5170 Yonge St., Willowdale, Ont. M2N 5T5

YES! I want to be one of the first to discover

Harlequin American Romance. Send me FREE and without
obligation *Twice in a Lifetime.* If you do not hear from me after I
have examined my FREE book, please send me the 4 new
Harlequin American Romances each month as soon as they
come off the presses. I understand that I will be billed only $2.25
for each book (total $9.00). There are no shipping or handling
charges. There is no minimum number of books that I have to
purchase. In fact, I may cancel this arrangement at any time.
Twice in a Lifetime is mine to keep as a FREE gift, even if I do not
buy any additional books. 154 BPA NAZJ

Name	(please print)	
Address		Apt. no.
City	State/Prov.	Zip/Postal Code

Signature (If under 18, parent or guardian must sign.)

This offer is limited to one order per household and not valid to current Harlequin
American Romance subscribers. We reserve the right to exercise discretion in
granting membership. If price changes are necessary, you will be notified. Offer

AMR-SUB-2